First published by JMH World Publishing in 2018
This edition published in 2018 by JMH World Publishing
Copyright © JM Hart 2018
jmhartwriter.com
The moral right of the author has been asserted.

The Emerald Tablet: Immersion
EPUB: 9781925786170
Cover design by Juan Padron
Publishing services provided by Critical Mass
www.critmassconsulting.com

IMMERSION

BOOK TWO IN THE EMERALD TABLET SERIAL

JM HART

JMH WORLD PUBLISHING

ABOUT IMMERSION BOOK TWO IN THE EMERALD TABLET SERIES

Shaun wishes he could go back in time to fix the past. A decade after his father unlocked a mysterious tomb and unleashed a mind-controlling virus; humanity continues to fight a losing battle. Shaun, confused and alone, runs to the only place he feels comfortable; the city.

Walking the city streets at night, he quickly realizes that the infected are out of control; randomly killing pedestrians, and smashing everything in sight. It's not safe, not even for him. It's only a matter of days until martial law is declared. A riot breaks out, and buildings are set ablaze. Shaun can do nothing, but watch the city burn.

But the cynical teen's last spark of hope flares when he sees two incredible guys step through a portal and disappear. He needs to find out how they did it, and maybe he can stop the apocalypse.

Immersion is the second episode in the action-packed

supernatural dystopian urban fantasy series The Emerald Tablet filled with daring teens, page-turning adventures, and otherworldly powers.

I dedicate this book to my daughter Bianca – never stop dreaming.

It is better to conquer yourself than to win a thousand battles.
Then the victory is yours.

Buddha

METATRON: CASEY. ENGLAND

Casey sat on a fallen branch, scanning the silver birch trees. They hid him and the house from the road. He rubbed his palms on his denim jeans and cleared his mind, trying to connect to Sophia, when from between the trees a sandy-colored Labrador stepped into view. "Here girl." The dog ran straight to him and licked him on the face. Casey shuffled the leaves at his feet for a stick. He picked one up, placed it across his knee and snapped it in two. He threw the longest piece of the stick into the air and obediently the dog fetched. Casey threw it again and again the dog retrieved it. "No more, girl. I need to think." The dog kept pushing the stick with her nose. "No, I need to focus on my friend Sophia. Go home." The dog picked up the stick and again dropped it at Casey's feet. He eyed the dog, and then the stick. He began to visualize it lifting off the ground — and it lifted. Not very high, but it hovered. He flicked his head to the side, making his curls bounce, and the stick went sailing up into the air. Like a rubber band it retracted, smacking him in the face. "Shit!" He dabbed under his eye. He tried again. He connected with the stick and imagined it soaring through the air, then flicked his head up and to the side. The stick flew into the bushes. The Labrador bounded after it. Casey's head hurt; he rubbed his temples, the pain was minimal, but an electric sensation above his eyes travelled down his face and his lips became itchy.

Out of the woods came the dog, drooling with the stick in its mouth.

"Yuk, I'm not touching that."

"Casey, you want to come and help me?"

Casey looked over his shoulder. Terry was hanging out the back door. He turned to the dog and with a slight movement of his eyes and a tilt of his head, he lifted the stick and tossed it into the air. "Fetch," he said. The stray Labrador mirrored Casey and tilted his head. Casey glanced over his shoulder at Terry. "Sure, Terry, give me a sec," he yelled back. He picked up the stick with his hand this time, and tossed it towards the hedges and the dog started to lumber after it. The ground vibrated. The Labrador stood still and began to howl.

"What is it, girl?" Through the narrow parting in the trees, a series of army trucks shot past in a blur of camouflage-green. "It's starting, girl. It's the virus. Hell's circus has come to town. Come on, girl, you look like you could use some water." Casey headed over to Terry at the house.

"Who's your friend?" Terry asked.

"She came out of the trees." Casey turned on the tap and the dog lapped it up. He jerked his head to the road. "Where do you think they're heading?"

"Town, probably."

Terry rested his hand on Casey's shoulder. "Come on. Come give me a hand downstairs. Maybe give her something to eat first. She's looking a little thin. Give her a couple of powdered eggs and the sausages left from last night."

"Wait here, girl," Casey said.

The dog sat, its tail dusting the ground.

The kitchen was freshly painted. It was looking new except for the moldy section that grew up the side of the wall.

"Where's Amy?" Casey continued to mix the egg powder and water in a bowl.

"In the cellar."

"What are you guys doing down there, anyway? And isn't it called a basement?"

"Sorting through her great-aunt's old treasures. Some of the things are actually amazing. I have a hunch that the dampness in the kitchen wall began down there."

Casey took the bowl out to the dog. "I'll meet you downstairs."

At the sight of the bowl the dog stood, a whimper escaped its mouth and saliva hung from the corner. It tapped its paw, wanting to step forward, then barked. Casey put the bowl on the grass and the dog buried her head in it. "That will keep you going for a while."

"Terry! Do you want me to bring the toolbox?" he yelled.

"Why are you shouting?"

"Ha ha. I thought you had already gone downstairs."

The stairs creaked as Terry descended ahead of Casey and the light bulb swung overhead. Amy was sitting on one of the many trunks, absorbed in unpacking another. Terry looked as though his heart fluttered when he looked at Amy. Casey knew she was his touchstone in life: they would fall apart without each other.

The air was thick and moist in the cellar. "You shouldn't be down here in your condition," Terry said.

"Ah!" Amy jumped off the trunk, arm up ready for attack. "Don't creep up on me! You guys here to do some real work or just scare the hell out of me?"

"Okay, no need for sarcasm, madam. What's with the kung fu moves?" Terry said, chopping the dust with his hands.

"He's right, Amy. Mold would be thriving in this atmosphere and it's not good for your lungs."

"It's not good for any of our lungs," Terry said. "Why don't you pick which trunk you want to go through next and we will lug it upstairs to the sunroom for you?"

"Well, I don't know. It's a lot of work for you."

"We'll have to cart the stuff upstairs that you want to throw out or sell. You might as well sort it out up there," Terry said.

"Who are we going to sell it to? There's hardly anyone around," Casey said.

"Don't be so negative, okay. I'm finishing this one now. It's full of beautiful old clothes. Turn-of-the-century stuff. You can take those old trunks against the far wall, behind the stairs, over there." She pointed. "Those ones are also ready to go."

Casey moved over to the trunks. Examining them, he could feel the energy of the past saturating the wood.

Casey sat next to Amy on the leather chest that smelt like a worn saddle.

"The room was filled with priceless memories," she said. "Think of the people who must have worn these clothes years and years ago. The dinner parties, balls, formal courting. How romantic it must have been."

Casey saw her aura expanding, as she imagined her family's past.

"Did you see the cot, Terry? It's to die for. It's so old — and that desk chair, look how worn that seat is."

"Yep, a lot of backsides have been in that chair. Maybe your great-uncle, with a pipe in one hand and a whiskey in the other, spinning the odd yarn to guests," Terry said.

"You're mocking me? You know, all of this stuff should really go upstairs. The air down here will damage it eventually. I'm surprised it's not already covered in mold. God knows how it has survived."

Three trunks were stacked up high against the wall. "We are going to need a ladder. I'll get it," Casey said, mounting the stairs two at time.

The back door slammed and the dog stood at attention, wagging its tail. "You still here? Don't you have a home? Isn't there someone missing you, girl?" Casey asked. "Come on, then."

They both stopped a few steps from the barn and the dog growled. "What's the matter, girl. Afraid of a few rats?"

The decaying wooden door hung unevenly with one corner wedged into the grass. "It will need to be fixed, girl, but not right now." Casey gave it a couple of good yanks and it opened. Instantly, he saw the ladder hiked up on the side wall. He reached up to unhook it, but lost his grip, the ladder crashed to the floor, landing a hair's breadth away from the dog. "Sorry girl, I — what the hell!" A black mist of tiny insects, like a thousand fruit flies, swarmed down from the rafters and encircled him. He coughed and choked. They went up his nostrils and down the back of his throat. Pain exploded in Casey's head. He grabbed his hair and doubled over gagging, vomiting up his lunch. His body was on fire, his head hammering. Tiny claws dug into the sinus cavities up his nose, the fastest route to the brain. His ears and nose bled. "Oh, God!" He released an agonized scream as his eyes turned black like swirling pools of oil. His mouth stretched wide, his jaw unhinged, and the black vileness travelled to his brain.

Casey fought for control. The barn came alive with projectiles and the dog ran.

An explosion of intense blinding light filled the barn and everything stopped in mid-air and collapsed to the ground. A figure, which stood three times the size of a man, emerged from the center of the light. It had three sets of wings unfolding behind him: from his shoulder blades, from the middle of his spine, and a set from just below his waist. They sparkled with trails of misty light. The lower right wing gracefully extended and swooped down, catching Casey and rolling him up, squeezing him tight, pressing out his last breath until all the devil's vermin was expelled from his body, freeing Casey from the virus. The heavenly being held him tight until the demons were crushed and vaporized.

Casey felt no pain as his bones were crushed. The angel's touch was gentle, its illumination was blinding. He couldn't look into its face, his eyelids sealed tight and in Casey's mind's eye he saw a rainbow enclosing them. In a partially conscious state, in that feeling of being between sleep and wakefulness, just before the sensation of falling, Casey saw his mom. No oxygen left in his body, he smiled back at his mom while the wings unfolded two at a time, lowering Casey to the dusty floor of the old barn. He heard the dog move. Casey imagined it was listening, tilting its head to the left and to the right. The dog barked in the distance, running to the house. Casey, not breathing, moved towards his mother.

The angel gently laid down Casey's head. "Metatron, my name is Metatron."

THE BARKING ECHOED into the house and down the stairs. Terry and Amy looked at each other for a second, then together they ran for the stairs. "Casey," Amy yelled. The sound of the step splintering under her foot was like bones breaking to Terry. She lost her balance. Reaching for him, she felt her fingers skim his shirt. Terry stretched out to catch her but missed and Amy fell over the edge of the stairs landing on the hard dirt floor.

"Amy!" He raced back downstairs.

The wind knocked out of her, she struggled to breathe. She spoke between breaths. "I'm ... okay. It's ... Casey. I know it ... go!" She pulled herself up awkwardly.

Terry ran up and outside. The dog headed in the direction of the barn.

"Oh no, dear God, no," Terry mumbled. Casey was on the ground with blood coming out of his nose. Terry's mouth went dry, his heart raced. The horror of the first time he'd seen Casey lying motionless came flooding back and he was afraid. Terry got down on his knees and placed his hand on the boy's chest — nothing; he put his ear to his mouth — nothing. A tear escaped from the corner of Terry's eye and dripped onto Casey's neck. Terry waited to feel the warmth of his breath — nothing.

"Terry. What's happening, what's wrong with him?" Out of breath, Amy crouched opposite him.

Terry ignored Amy's quivering voice and began resuscitation. *Compressions, one breath, compressions, another breath, compressions, another breath, ...* He kept repeating the mantra inside his head.

The sound of Casey coughing and choking was bliss.

Terry turned him on his side. Casey coughed up blood and spat.

Amy brushed his hair out of his eyes. "What happened?"

Casey looked pasty; exhausted, he managed to push out a smile. He watched them fuss over him. He lifted his head up. Amy gently pushed it back down and moved his hair out of his eyes.

"Don't try to get up, wait a few minutes," she said. "Think it's about time you had a haircut, mister. You're a mangy poodle." Amy's attention was drawn to the lofty heights of the barn. "I never noticed how much light there was in here. I bet the rafters would be filled with secrets."

Casey lifted himself to his elbows and slowly sat up, breathing deeply. His chest expanded, filling with air, triggering a fit of coughing.

"Take it easy, pal," Terry said crouched beside him.

Once the coughing stopped he took in a couple of deliberately short breaths. His body wasn't satisfied, and independently took in consecutive rapid shallow breaths. He looked as if he had bottled up the tears of a lifetime and breathed out in a heavy sigh.

"My mouth tastes terrible." He snorted back blood from his nose and spat. "I feel like I have just gone twelve rounds in the boxing ring." He massaged his cheeks and said, "My jaw's stiff, and my ear is throbbing."

"And you don't remember what happened? You gave us a hell of a fright!" Amy said.

"I'm not sure. I opened the door, grabbed the ladder, then my head exploded.

After that, I don't remember."

Terry held out his hand and Casey looked up. "Ready to stand, pal?"

"Yeah, yeah sure." He steadied himself against Terry. He

wanted to just hug him and bury his head into Terry's chest and sob. But he couldn't; he was supposed to be grown-up now. He had had hairy armpits for the past year, and his voice had matured. *Then why do I feel like a terrorized little kid?* he mused. They both helped him walk back to the house and into the kitchen. The dog followed, settling in to sit by the door.

～

"WELL, GOOD MORNING," Amy said, a little too chirpy, turning off the computer screen. "You slept well. Grab yourself a bowl of cereal and come downstairs when you're ready. I'm off to sort out those last few items. We're going to have a great garage sale when the world gets back on its feet."

"What are you doing on the computer that you don't want me to see, Amy?"

"Nothing. Nothing really."

She looked embarrassed, avoiding his eyes as she glanced out the window.

"What am I doing? This isn't like me," she said and looked him in the eyes. "I was just watching the online news. It feels like we are cocooned out here and I want it to stay that way. I want to protect you from the chaos out there." She flicked her head towards the window.

"You can't protect me, not really."

"But we have to keep trying. I saw you with my book the other night."

"Which one?"

"Don't play dumb, you're no good at it," she said, pulling her long hair into a scruffy ponytail. "My grandfather's leather book of splendor."

"Sorry, I should have asked."

"I don't mind. I don't own it, I'm just the caretaker. You're welcome to meditate on it anytime. I know you speak Aramaic too."

Casey laughed. "I know, right. And I feel something, I really do — I don't know how come. When I hold it, when I open it, I become transfixed on the letters. I'm pulled into its energy, I don't know how to describe it. My body relaxes, I feel calm. It's like somewhere inside me a treasure box is flung open and sparkling sapphires, rubies, emeralds and diamonds radiate through my body. I feel illuminated in gold dust, and my eyes are filled with a scintillating light. I feel close to God — to all things, as if the universe is cradling me."

"Wow. That's amazing! Were your parents religious?"

"No, I haven't even been baptized."

"Have you ever read the Bible, Torah, or Qur'an?"

"I read the Bible a little when we were in the hospital. There was nothing else to read."

"I think God has his eye on you, Casey."

"There's something else though."

"What's that? You can tell me anything, Casey, honestly."

He paused. Should I tell her about the experience of drowning in the river, or about my ability to see auras, or that I can move objects with my mind? Can she help me? God, I wish she could. But she has enough just surviving, and now the pregnancy. I'm not her kid, I'm not her responsibility. Sophia will help me."

"Casey, what is it?"

"Um, nothing. Let's just finish watching the news together."

He turned the computer screen on. Amy watched him sit on the side of the old table, dressed in denim jeans and a white t-shirt. "That shirt is getting too tight around the arms for you." She patted his leg, letting him know everything was okay.

On the screen, the reporter standing in the middle of a street tried to make an announcement, while looters ran around in the background. The tall buildings blocked the sun casting a grey haze across the reporter's face. "The USA has closed its borders," he said. "All planes have been grounded and the airports have been closed. Cruise ships are being denied the right to dock for supplies. The death toll has tripled and is rising. We are annihilating ourselves. Who said we would *nuke* ourselves, blow ourselves to smithereens? Forget about the threat from other countries, the battle is within each and every one of us. What is the government doing? Where is the vaccination we were promised? Where has Professor Ellen Freeman and her promising vaccine gone? Has all this madness been an engagement in biological warfare? These are the questions on everyone's —"

The reporter ducked. Gunfire filled the streets; looters were shooting shopfront windows and setting rubbish bins alight. The reporter composed himself and pushed his earpiece into his ear. "It has just been reported that the National Guard will now close New York City. I have been advised to stop broadcasting and leave the area immediately but —" His shirt puffed with a breath of air before it changed to crimson. He seized his stomach, looked into the camera, and painfully stated, "I've been shot." The cameraman swung around to where the shots had been fired from, and through the lens the world was eyeballing the smoking barrel of a gun.

Violently, the gun was pulled back, turned around and the butt of the gun was smashed against the camera's optics, cracking the glass as the soldier yelled, "SHUT THAT

DOWN, SHUT THAT DOWN — NOW!" The screen went blank.

Amy had her hand at her throat. "God help them; help them all."

"You just saw what they did, Amy. Why would you say that?" Casey, not waiting for an answer, left the room.

⁓

CASEY SAT ALONE on the back step in the morning sun, shuffling his cereal around with his spoon. *The soy milk still tastes like cardboard.* He looked up to see the Labrador running out of the barn.

"Hey, girl, are you hungry? I've got a half-eaten bowl of cereal with your name on it." He left the bowl on the step and went inside, down to the basement.

"Morning, pal," Terry said. "You up for this?"

"Sure, lay it on me." Casey's throat was sore and his head felt a little light. But otherwise, he felt fine.

They both lifted the top trunk down and could see the mold on its back. Amy inspected each one, dragging her hand along the surface as if stroking an elegant stallion. "If you guys could take both of these upstairs, that would be good."

"Terry, what's this?" Casey asked.

"Its mold. It's also along this support beam. The wall is stone. Something has to be causing the dampness. Casey, help me with this last trunk." Together they shuffled it away from the wall, exposing a hole. A few select stones were missing, which had created an opening the size of a small dog.

"That's the biggest rat hole I've ever seen," Amy said, trying to lighten the tension that had suddenly entered the basement. "Pass me the torch, Amy," Terry said, putting his hand out behind him.

"Can you see anything?" Casey asked.

Terry was lying face down on the dirt floor peering into the hole. "It looks like there might be a chamber beyond the wall, a tunnel maybe. I've read there are tunnels all around here that were used for walking secretively between different properties, like lords meeting their mistresses, or hiding loot from thieves. The Cleeves Cove cave system is north-west of here. Shh, I can hear dripping."

"You're the only one talking, sweetie."

Amy and Casey smirked at each other, shook their heads and rolled their eyes. They crowded around Terry, trying to get a look. "We'll have to make the entrance wider. Wide enough for us to crawl through and take a good look."

"I'm not crawling anywhere," Amy said, losing interest. "I'm happy with the trunks. You two can go crawling through a maze of tunnels, but I'm going to go make us some lunch."

"I'm feeling a little tired," Casey said. "I wouldn't mind some downtime."

"I CAN SMELL THE FOREST, how come I smell the forest? Can you smell my room? It's got a musty smell. That old-grandma smell," Casey said.

"Don't freak, okay?" Sophia whispered.

"Okay, but why would I freak?"

"I can't smell your room, because you are visiting me this time. You came here, you came to me. This is really good, Casey, but you can't leave your body unprotected. You're a flame to moths, and you don't want the kind of moths that are fluttering around the world at the moment."

"This feels terrific. If I look down, I can't see my body. It's like I am awake within my sleeping self."

"You are really changing, Casey. This is the last time we will be able to communicate for a while. We're moving on — it's time for me to leave the cabin. Next time we talk it will be in the flesh."

"You remind me of Amy. Your confidence — she has such confidence that this virus will blow over and everything will be okay. You even look a little like her, you know."

"Her thinking is resilient, mine is not so." Sophia's tone deepened. "Casey, I have wanted to be with my family, and the only time I can do that is when I am asleep or astral traveling. Astral travel isn't the healthiest thing, living in this reality. I have been selfish and have wanted to die. Amy is selfless and tough. I am learning to be strong."

"Do you still want to die?"

"My best friends were gunned down. Mother Catherine, who I loved as if she was my own mother, died a painful death to save me. But no, I don't want to die."

"There's a lot to live for Sophia. I'm your friend. The universe wants us here for a reason. It wants us to want to live. I was saved from the flood and you were saved from the fire. We have to keep going. I know things are pretty crazy. We went into town last week to get supplies for the next few months: buckets of protein powder, tinned food, a whole bunch of stuff, and we saw some infected people."

"How're the headaches?"

"Pretty good. The more I practice, the less it hurts. I can move things as long as they're not too heavy, otherwise I get a killer headache. It's actually starting to be fun."

"Learn to reverse the energy flow."

"What do you mean?"

"Instead of projecting your energy onto an external object, use it to propel yourself. Use the Earth's gravity to your advantage; like the opposite pole of a magnet. Flip yourself between the two to draw things near, or propel. Imagine you can create your own flying carpet."

"Flying carpet, that sounds a little nuts."

"Well, maybe not a flying carpet. Jet streams of energy from the soles of your feet, like a rocket, might be more like it. You can do it. The question is: do you want to do it? You're fading. Casey?"

"I can feel myself awakening, I can hear Amy and Terry talking. Bye, Sophia. I'll be waiting. I hope you're real. God, I hope you're real."

2

FRENZY OF FLIES: JADE. AUSTRALIA

It was time to leave the parallel world and Jade shuffled as close as possible to the membrane and placed her hand against it, feeling the coolness. It reminded her of her mother's lab, the agar jelly she would find in a petri dish. When Jade was younger, she had loved to watch the bacteria multiply. *The wall is moving, it's a living energy. It feels thin and pliable,* she was thinking as she felt the pulsing, magnetic field. She pushed her arm through until her fingertips could feel the breeze on the other side.

"Come on, let's go." Tim went through, then Jade and Kevin followed behind.

Jade put her hand to her mouth as soon as she was on the other side. "What's that stench?" A frenzy of flies buzzed around swollen carcasses. "The poor things, they're kangaroos. Where are we?"

"Back in everyday reality," Tim said, "where everything has about one per cent of the color of the other world we just left."

Jade looked around at the burnt landscape. It looked like shades of grey in comparison to where they had been.

Tim babbled on in her ear, his shoulders slumped. "It's where people don't give a shit about each other, and the almighty plague is upon us. It's depressing actually."

"No, I mean what country?"

"Australia," Kevin said. "Where do you think you are?"

"Home. Myrtle Beach."

"You live in a resort at the Gold Coast?"

Jade looked at Tim as if he had two heads. "No. I don't even know where the Gold Coast is," she snapped.

"You're from the States, aren't you? You don't live around here at all," Kevin said. "We just walked from one end of the world to the other, didn't we?"

"I must be still drugged. I must be ... still in the cabin in the woods!" *That's right, I was kidnapped and woke up feeling cold. There was a black hooded jacket over a chair in the corner. I took it and ran.* She touched her head — no cuts, no pain, but there was dried blood matted in her hair, a bruise on her arm and a needle mark. "You got a cell I can use?" she asked, rubbing her arms.

"You mean a mobile. Nah, sorry," Kevin said.

Thrusting her head forward and raising her voice, she said, "Everyone has a phone!"

"Then where's yours?" Tim said.

"Look, there's no point standing around arguing. Let's get back to my place and you can use my mom's phone."

Jade started scratching, feeling tiny pricks against her skin, and her stomach somersaulted. It was nerves. The atmosphere between them had changed. They no longer had an internal dialogue. *The effects of the quantum world were wearing off.* The day had become gloomy.

"We had mobiles, but our parents snatched them because we ran up a hefty bill of twelve hundred bucks. We use prepaid now and never have any credit. Can only receive calls, so what's the point in carrying them around?" Kevin explained.

"I couldn't live without mine," Jade said.

"Let me guess," Tim said. "You're one of those girls always texting her friend who is standing right next to her, and posting online what she had for breakfast, and how beautiful her hair smelt with the new shampoo Mommy bought from some flash department store."

"No! I use it for research, watching university lectures on YouTube and I can calculate mathematical formulas with it."

"We have to cross the river. At this time of the day it's only about knee-deep," Kevin said. The sky was filled with the same grey clouds and the air was suffocating, with the same humidity that the boys experienced before they had disappeared.

"Is it always this hot in Australia?"

"It's hot, but not usually at this time of year. Queensland wears that crown," Kevin said.

"What happened here?"

"There was a fire a few days ago; some assholes with petrol bombs. They stole our bikes and left us for dead," Tim said.

"And that's when the wall first appeared," Kevin said.

The guys pushed their bikes over the flat anthill, yards away from where Shaun had been waiting for them two days ago. They came out of the bush and a dead dog lay in the gutter. Its head looked like an exploding watermelon and it had begun to rot.

"This place gives me the creeps. Why do you hang out here?"

"It's not normally like this," Kevin said.

They silently continued on. Not a single car passed by, and only one kid coasted down the street on his board.

"Where is everyone?" Jade asked.

"The virus," Kevin said.

"It hasn't hit this bad at home — well, it didn't appear to be this bad. We always seem to have some massacre happening anyway, some degraded moron taking innocent lives. Maybe we have been infected for years and it's like bamboo." She stopped and put her hand over her mouth. She couldn't believe her own attitude. "That was very obnoxious of me."

"Ob — what? and what's bamboo got to do with anything?" Tim said.

"Nasty, I was being really nasty." She rolled her eyes. "Bamboo is invasive; it proliferates above and underground — seen and unseen — spreading to unwanted areas. It's tough to eradicate, like a nasty virus spreading unseen through our bodies. Lucky your name only has three letters," she said to Tim. "Oh, sorry, that was nasty too." She pressed her fingers against her head as if it hurt.

"It's been pretty crazy lately," Kevin said, looking sideways at her, confused at the sudden change. "We thought the virus would pass us by, but it hasn't, it has created millions of psychopaths."

"In the emergency waiting area last night, we watched a man break his wife's arm so she could see a doctor. Kevin foresaw it, and charged at the man. He was too late and copped a backhand."

Jade looked at Kevin, trying to see his face. He tilted his head, letting his fringe drop into his eyes, and looking down at the road. He stepped up his pace and stared at the road ahead. He reminded her of the way she had been before her mom went missing. She'd always tried to hide behind her hair, in case someone saw how she really felt.

"HEY, retards, yeah you! I want to talk to you."

Kevin looked up. Across the street Shaun swung his legs over the side of the roof.

"Why are you walking in the middle of the road? Who's the girl? She looks pretty messed up."

"Run," Tim said.

They bolted down the road and around the corner, turning off at Stewart Avenue. Along Kevin's street red and blue lights reflected off the windows and he could see a police car parked out front of his house. Kevin went to run inside, but stopped. Suddenly he was filled with dread. He became worried for his family; he was scared something had happened. It brought back the memories when his grandparents died.

Kevin and Tim stood shoulder to shoulder. "Shit, dude, what the hell's going on?"

Kevin focused and searched inside the house with his mind, feeling for the emotions. "It's about us. Your mom is in there too, she's crying. Kath's pissed off and she's holding Molly who is crying. Let's go."

"It's about us?" Tim said. "I feel like Tom Sawyer and Huck Finn."

Jade looked at Kevin suspiciously. "Why would you think you are in trouble?"

The trio walked up the porch. Kevin watched Jade let her hair down to cover her face as he opened the front door. Everything happened so quickly. Alex ran to him and wrapped his arms around his legs. His mother started yelling at him. He looked at his dad who was showing a school photo of Kevin and Tim. The scent of sage and lemongrass wafted past him, he felt relieved. *Nanna is here.*

Tim's mother was on the sofa with a box of tissues. She jumped up for joy at the sight of him. The tissues fell off her lap as she raced over to Tim and held him tight. His faced was buried in her chest and Kevin thought Tim would suffocate if she didn't let him go soon.

Nobody had noticed the barefoot girl beside him. Kevin was worried Jade would run. He could sense her hiding, peeking into the room, watching his mother yelling at him. He was embarrassed, his face turned red. She was rough and squeezed his shoulders demanding to know where they had been. Kevin had never known her to touch him aggressively, but supposed it was as close to a hug as he was going to get.

As soon as the boys walked in, Molly had settled down. Kath gently placed her in the playpen and laid the bunny rug over her before making her way to her brother. She pulled him from her mother's clutches and pretended to be glad to see him. She hugged him, and whispered in his ear. Tim's mother pulled him back into a bear hug as soon as Kath let go. Crying and thanking God for returning her son.

Tim's voice was muffled as he yelled, "Ma, I can't breathe."

Kevin tried to wriggle out of his mother's grip, but she wasn't letting go yet. Daniel stepped in between Kevin and Callie and hugged him. Kevin wanted to collapse into his arms and cry. He wished his dad would never let him go. *Keep it together,* he said to himself, feeling his body ready to drop. He stepped back and looked up at his dad and quietly said, "We found a girl. She's at the front door and won't come into the room."

"What?" Daniel looked up, saw Jade and was at her side in a few strides. He looked back at Kevin, then guided Jade gently into the room.

Everyone looked at Jade as she entered the room, concerned at her appearance. "Where have you boys been?" the policeman asked, quickly moving to Jade. "And is that blood in your hair?" He pulled a pair of gloves from his pocket and examined her head. "There doesn't seem to be any wounds. Did these boys hurt you?"

Jade just kept staring at Kevin's mom, and his mom looked at Kevin with a dumbfounded expression, then she looked at Jade, confused. *What are they both thinking?* Kevin wondered.

"But how the ...?" Callie walked over to Jade and pushed her hair away from her face. Kevin watched Jade stare at his mother, her eyes filling with tears. His mom pulled Jade into a reassuring embrace and comforted her. He himself hadn't felt that from her in a very long time.

Kath leant in between Tim and Kevin and said as loud as she dared, "You've been gone for nearly three days."

Kevin and Tim didn't understand what was happening, but they both knew the police had to go. "We're scared to walk the streets with so many psychos wandering around," Tim said, drawing their attention. "So we went bush. That's when we found Jade. She had fallen down an embankment. It was getting dark and we were lost so we made camp. The next day we started out together when the sun came up and kept walking; we were going in circles and extremely thirsty. I thought I was going to have to drink my own urine. Luckily, we found the fire trail, though home was still far away and it was getting dark. We had to stop for the night for fear of getting lost again."

Kevin looked at the adults, wondering if they thought

Tim believable. *What was the part about drinking his urine? He is mind-blowingly nuts.*

Kath spoke first. "So why did you take the bikes?"

"That's not important," Tim said.

"That doesn't make sense," Kath said.

"Now you two, stop your bickering," Tim's mom said.

Kevin wondered why the hell Tim was making up a story. He looked at his friend and raised his hands slightly as if to say, what gives?

Daniel cleared his throat and shook the officer's hands. "Well, mate, it looks like all is accounted for and then some. My wife obviously knows the girl. We'll see she gets home safely."

The policeman pulled his leather gloves from his pocket and turned to Kevin and Tim. "You guys are right to stay off the streets. The infected are outnumbering us these days, but stay close to home. Don't go hiking till this is over," he said, tilting his head towards the street.

Daniel and the policeman walked out of the room. "I'll be off then. A word of advice — The army will be moving tomorrow and there will be roadblocks in all capital cities to prevent people from leaving. Sixty-mile perimeter north, south, east and west and the docks are staying closed. Most people won't even know they have been boxed in. Orders are, shoot to kill. You didn't hear it from me."

"Seriously, that bad, huh?" Daniel said.

The policeman pulled out his sunglasses. "Well, it's happening. All the action at the moment is over at the hospital, which you're probably well aware of. So many people infected. It's crazy."

"Any sign of a vaccine?"

"No. No vaccine, no antivirals, and antibiotics are useless. The suicides are the worst. Heartbreaking — whole families sometimes. The world is going to hell. This job is getting harder every day. I am tired of meeting people when they are having the worst day of their lives. I'm glad it has turned out well on this occasion. You take good care of yours, keep your boy on a leash for a while. I think it's time I put in for some leave, if you know what I mean."

"Thanks, officer."

"Call me Bill." They shook hands again.

KEVIN WONDERED when his mom would let go of Jade, then Callie pulled back and held her at arm's-length. Jade started sobbing.

"Jade, how did you get here? You're safe. It will be alright." Callie pulled her back into her arms.

A waterfall of long, black hair fell forward and hid Jade's face from him. Kevin watched his mom protectively putting her arms around Jade again. *How did his mother know her name, and how does Jade know my mom?* He had so many questions. He went over to Tim. Before he could say anything Tim's mom shuffled him out of the room and to the front door.

"Home with you, boy," she said.

"You stink," Kath was saying as she passed Kevin. "Where have you been? I don't believe a word of your story."

Tim blurted out. "Ah, we were really helping Shaun. Mr D said to steer clear of Shaun. That's why we didn't say anything."

Kevin didn't know what to do or say. What the hell was Tim up to now?

"Who?" Tim's mom asked.

"Shaun, a friend of ours."

"Yeah, right," Kath said. "Since when has Shaun Grady been a friend of yours?" She placed her hands on her hips. She cocked her head and raised her eyebrows, daring him to answer.

Daniel walked over and tilted Kevin's head slightly back so their eyes met. He couldn't look away. "Is that true? You should have called. We were worried. Don't ever do that again — is Shaun alright?"

Kath looked confused as she watched Daniel speak to the guys as if he knew what they were babbling on about.

"He, his head ..." Kevin wasn't as quick as Tim in coming up with compelling stories and felt uncomfortable. "Shaun's head was hurting pretty badly and he didn't want to go back to hospital. We stayed until his dad came home. I thought Tim called his mom and she called you guys."

"That's right," Tim said, grinning at Kath. "But I thought Kevin called you, Mr D, and you called my mom."

Kevin tried to keep his emotions under control and he knew his dad was doing the same, knowing they were playing him. He was just as confused as everyone else about Callie and Jade. Kevin felt something was going on; he sensed it, and he knew someone would have to explain eventually. Right now, he was grateful they didn't question him any more.

"Is there anything else you want to tell us?" Daniel said.

"Sorry," Kevin said. Daniel gave him a look of disbelief.

"Come on, Tim, let's get you into a bath."

"I'm fifteen, Mom. I don't do baths."

Callie let go of Jade, but kept her close to her side as she said to Tim's mom, "Sally, if you like you are welcome to join us for dinner. Kath has the magic touch with Molly."

Kevin looked at Molly sleeping soundly in her playpen.

"Thanks, but we'd better head off. Don't want to be out

after dark. The storm clouds look nasty. Lord knows we need rain, but those clouds don't look ordinary. I'm just glad the boys are back." Callie followed them to the front door. Moths were dancing around the porch light.

"By the way love, the smell of the lemongrass and sage," Sally said. "Very humbling, nice choice under the circumstances."

Callie smiled and nodded in thanks, waving and closing the door behind them.

Tim shoved his head around the doorframe and shouted to Kevin, "Call me," then quickly pulled his head out of the way of the closing door.

"I don't have any aroma oils in the house. I'm assuming that's what she meant." Callie shook her head in confusion. "Anyway, Daniel, can you get dinner ready for Molly and Alex. We can have dinner and talk once the little ones have gone to bed. Kevin, go shower. You can use the main bathroom and Jade can use my en suite."

Kevin and Daniel looked at each other, not knowing what was going on or why she was being so nice. They both replied, "Sure."

Kevin looked at his mom fussing over Jade. How does she know Jade's name? I didn't tell her? Jade hasn't spoken. He was aware that his mom's behavior had nothing to do with him. He walked upstairs to his bedroom to get a fresh set of clothes when there was a knock on his door.

"Kevin, can Jade borrow a shirt and your green cargoes, please," his mother asked.

"Sure." Jade stood behind his mom and it was difficult for him to make eye contact with her. Her head was lowered, her eyes were swollen from crying. "Is Jade alright?"

"She'll be fine," Callie said.

"Mom, how do you know her name?" He passed her some clothing.

"Get yourself cleaned up and then we'll make our own pizzas and chat." She closed the door.

He heard his mom say, "Let me get this straight. You were swimming, knocked out, drugged and kidnapped? And you're wearing short shorts? That's not like you, Jade."

3

PESTILENCE'S FUSION: SOPHIA. SCOTLAND

T he time had come to travel south. Hiding in the highlands and meditating was over, although it had given Sophia and Casey time to connect while the universe aligned the stars. The essence of the forest was comforting, the sound and the freshness of the stream healing, and the view of the valley from the cabin was enlightening, but it was time to go. They were lucky to have stumbled upon it. Father McDonald and Sophia said their goodbyes and the eagle circled above them as they walked out of the forest.

Worn denim jeans, a beard, messy hair, a black t-shirt and a sports coat helped to disguise Father McDonald. He no longer wore his collar. He carried his Bible in his inner-left breast pocket. The days were still warm, the evenings cool, but summer had begun to fade. Ten o'clock at night and the sun had finally settled over Scotland. Depression hung over the city of Glasgow. Under the darkness of night they entered the town, and took a seat in the corner booth of a small cafe, keeping their heads low.

They watched the television, seeing angry protesters in

London demanding the fall of the monarchy. The next images were angry protesters in Rome surrounding the Vatican, demanding the removal of the Pope. From his balcony he appealed to the people before him to help each other, to love their neighbor, and promised they would find peace. They ignored his pleas, demanding he perform a public exorcism, claiming their loved ones were possessed by the devil. He tried to reassure them, advising them to stay in their homes and not to travel; the government would find a vaccine. Ceremoniously he released two white doves, the sign of peace, and the crowd went silent as the birds took flight. Then suddenly a burst of cheering rose from St Peter's Square as a crow swooped in and attacked the dove, dislodged white feathers drifting on the wind. A seagull joined the crow to attack the second dove. The cheers grew louder as the doves started to fall and the crow continued to peck at the Vatican's symbol of peace.

Horrified, Sophia and Father McDonald continued watching images from across the world of people lining up outside the churches, synagogues and mosques. "The people claim their loved ones who have been infected have become possessed by demons," the reporter announced from behind the safety of his desk, then broadcast the next set of horrific images across the screen. Homemade bombs hurtled through the air, exploding on the White House lawn.

Father McDonald looked over at Sophia. Tears were streaming down her face.

"Let's leave here," he said, holding his hand out to her.

They shuffled out of the booth as a picture of a younger Father McDonald and a young Sophia was splashed across the TV screen. The reporter accused Father McDonald of being a pedophile who had kidnapped Sophia, a young orphan girl, after shooting his parishioners.

They were both horrified and hurried from the cafe. The streets had become scary, so they looked for another place to eat and hide. The last cafe had stolen a little more of their light, and Sophia could see Father McDonald was weakening. They moved on, looking for a decent place that was open. They walked down dark narrow back streets that stank of urine and alcohol. Sophia kept away from the building walls, staying in the middle of the roads afraid of what might reach out of the shadows. A light was switched on up ahead, revealing three steps to a back door. They looked for a place to hide. Sophia stumbled over a pair of legs; the owner didn't flinch, not a sound. Sophia picked herself up. The door opened beneath the light: a silhouette, then a tall man emerged carrying a bag of trash, cigarette dangling from his mouth. He put down the garbage, inhaled on the cigarette and as he puffed, the smoke floated up to the light and the moths. He looked down into the alley, stepping in their direction.

Ducking behind a dumpster wasn't an option. Father McDonald's legs were liable to snap, so they kept walking. The man watched them go by. Father McDonald's hands were casually stuffed into his pockets and Sophia's hoodie was pulled up over her head. They kept their heads down, and cautiously passed him by.

"Hey, you two," the tall man said in a thick Scottish accent. "It looks like you could use a good meal. Come on in." He chucked his smoke to the ground and ground at it with his heel. He pulled the door open and held it for them.

The duo looked at each other, as if having a conversation only they could hear.

"Thank you," Father McDonald said. They walked into a

kitchen, entering the back of a cafe. "You and the wee hen can sit here." The man showed them to an empty table away from the others; no TV screen, low lighting and hardly anyone was in the place. Perfect.

"I'll be back." He came back with a coffee, a milkshake, hot fish and chips, toasted club sandwiches and a bottle of water.

"Thank you," Sophia said, pushing her sleeves up to her elbows.

"You're welcome, hen. It's a slow night, what can I say? It's mayhem out there. Where are you two headed? Trying to get out of the city, or did you just come down from them hills?" He couldn't help looking at Sophia. Strange young lady, he thought. Her eyes were constantly looking past him and over his shoulder as if he had something on his back. He turned and looked behind him, but there was nothing. She looked above his head and he too looked upwards. But there was nothing.

"We're heading south," Father McDonald said.

"What's south, that's not north? This whole country is about to be put to sleep and under lock and key."

"Why are you open? Why aren't you leaving?" Sophia asked.

"No point running, hen. The virus is everywhere. No purpose in leaving. What do you keep looking at, young lady? You're giving me the creeps. You're making my skin crawl."

"Seeing if you have the virus."

"You can tell?" He took a step forward and looked her square in the face.

"Yes," she said.

He glanced at Father McDonald. They didn't look like a pair of hustlers. "Well! Let's have it." Feeling uneasy, his heart started to race. His stomach boiled and churned, as if he had eaten a bucket of hot peppers. He was scared; he didn't want to be one of the infected. Last week he was elbow-deep mopping up the blood of his dear brother, an infected. They had shared the restaurant for twenty-five years and his brother had never missed a day, not even when his kid was being born. Last Wednesday, he didn't show. He didn't answer his home phone or his mobile. So, for the first time, Joe had closed up shop, went to his brother's house and banged on his door. Silence. He checked around the back, took the spare key from the top ledge and let himself in. The old black-and-white checked linoleum floor was now red and black. A bloody axe by his brother's side and a gun in his hand. His baby brother had removed his wife's head before shooting his son and biting down on the barrel of the gun.

"No. No, you don't have the virus," Sophia said and smiled.

He dropped to his knees; his hands clasped in prayer, he raised them to the ceiling. "Thank God!"

"Do you want to know why?"

"Sophia!" Father McDonald warned.

"Sure, maybe I can prevent someone else from getting it. Maybe it's my blood type or something."

"That's why. Because you think of others first, and you think that there is good in everyone. Last year you were in a motorbike accident, weren't you? Drunken joy riders lost control and cut you off. Your leg was crushed between your bike and their car. You freed yourself and, dragging your crushed leg along the road, around to the other side of the car, you checked on the others. The driver was breathing. You smelt fumes, but you didn't stop. You reached up, opened his door and dragged him out. Seconds later, the car exploded, scorching your face. You lost your leg. You have a prosthesis attached to your knee, and still you don't hold a grudge. You believe there is a reason for everything. I could go on, but I think you get the message." She smiled gently. He was standing with his mouth open in amazement. He wasn't sure what to say or do; everything she said was correct.

"Who are you, a psychic? What's my past got to do with me not catching the virus?"

"The virus affects the brain. It is a small evil parasite that feeds off negative thoughts. When we get angry or scared, we create a different energy. They feed on fear, rage, pride, jealousy, envy and anger. Simple."

"The Evil Eye. That's why I wear this," he said, pointing to the string around his wrist. "My mother put it on me when I was a wee 'un and every time it fell off she would put a new one on. I continued to put it on after my bar mitzvah. I always wear my watch over it. I made the choice to keep wearing it even though we stopped going to the synagogue. My mother was asked to leave because she refused to stop studying her father's way of teaching, which was reserved for men over forty. She told me it was what her dad's father taught him, and he taught her, and they had continued to study even after they left Israel. The string is a protection, a reminder to be good — not to judge others or bring shame upon them, and to look towards God for guidance. Treat others how you would like to be treated, she always said. 'Life is too short.' So I always wear the red string. Wait, I have some for you." He pushed his way through the swinging door and they watched it move back and forth. Within a few swings he emerged with a tiny packet. He opened it up, mumbled a blessing, and tied it to Sophia's left wrist. He did the same for Father McDonald. He then held their hands together and prayed.

"Thank you, you're very kind," Father McDonald said. "God bless you."

"If you like, you can stay the night here."

"Thank you, but we don't want to put you to any trouble."

"Shouldn't you be telling someone in authority what you know about the virus?"

"It won't save people from themselves," Father McDonald said. "The authorities will just think she is a crazy young girl, some religious nut and lock us both up. I've learnt to let God guide Sophia — as much as I've wanted to end her pain and confusion."

People in the restaurant were looking at them suspiciously — or was it his paranoia? "Wrap that up and bring it with us," Father McDonald said.

Sophia unfolded a napkin and wrapped her unfinished sandwich, sucked back the rest of her milkshake, and stuffed her hot chips into the empty waxed cardboard cup, putting it under her jacket.

"How much do we owe you?"

"Nothing. It's on me. Call me Joe."

"Thanks, Joe, and may God bless you. Come on, Sophia."

They flipped up the hoods on their jackets and stuffed their hands in their pockets. They stepped out of the cafe to hide amongst the very thing that was seeking them out in the dead of the night: the dark, swarming invisible mist. It moved amongst the motorists, floating through open car windows, circulating amongst the passengers, up nostrils and into open mouths. Sophia watched in horror. Families began to argue as the virus impregnated their bodies, spreading across the brain, killing off neurons and consuming their souls.

Cars suddenly screeched to a stop, drivers and passengers jumped out yelling obscenities. Sophia and Father McDonald hid in the shadows. The brawl escalated, affecting oncoming traffic. Another car screeched to a halt. Men and women jumped out of their vehicles and randomly started beating into each other. Bystanders watched; some seemed to enjoy the violence. A few horrified people looked down at their shoes and walked briskly away. No white flags were raised, no sirens wailed.

"Maybe we should go back to Joe's and wait till morning. It's harder to see the swarm in the dark. We can leave at first light?" Sophia said.

"Agreed. Let's go." They headed back to Joe's cafe, but the sign said "closed". Sophia and Father McDonald turned to leave when Joe flicked on the lights.

"I figured you might come back. It's a little rough out there. It smells a hell of a lot worse than usual. I have an apartment upstairs, come." They followed Joe into the back of the cafe, up an old narrow staircase that led into his apartment above.

"May I use the bathroom, please?" Sophia asked.

"Second door on the left, hen."

"You can sleep on the couch if that is okay. I'll make up a bed on the floor for your granddaughter. She is very gifted," Joe said as Sophia closed the bathroom door.

"Sophia is very blessed. The couch is more than enough, thank you."

BEFORE FIRST LIGHT, they delicately walked downstairs

trying to avoid any squeaky steps, careful not to wake Joe. They wanted to evade any offer for them to stay for breakfast. Father McDonald left a thank-you note and promised to keep him in their prayers. The bell on the front door jingled when the door opened and they closed it behind them. The street was quiet and an early morning fog was lifting. A few yards away a crow was walking over a dead body, a victim of the night. The crow behaved as if inspecting the carcass before purchase. Another crow landed on the dead man. The two crows cawed at Sophia and Father McDonald's approach, making their claim, eyeballing them. The empty street intensified the noise of the birds. Father McDonald couldn't walk past the body. He stopped, shooed away the birds and prayed for the man's soul. He took his Bible out and opened the book randomly. Sophia stood next to him with her hands by her side. "The word of the Lord came again unto me, saying, Son of man, set your face against the Ammonites, and prophesy against them; And say unto the Ammonites, Hear the word of the Lord God; Thus says the Lord God; Because you said, Aha, against my sanctuary, when it was profaned; and against the land of Israel ..."

A light began to glow around the body and the crows took flight. An ethereal body slowly, painfully, separated from the man's physical being, crouching on one knee and ripping itself away from the body. Sophia, feeling the man's pain, allowed her aura to expand and her energy to feed his soul with her light. The spirit of the man broke free from the chains of his physical body and his spiritual essence stood tall. He looked back at his body lying in the street, beaten, bloody, discarded. He turned to Father McDonald and nodded thanks and floated into the sky.

They watched him ascend, his soul sparkling like a

million stars. It soared up into the gorgeous colors of the morning sky. Suddenly, a swarm of blackness appeared from behind the buildings and descended on the man's ascending soul. She felt the pain of the man's soul, as they dominated it, pulling it apart, fighting each other for a piece of its light until his spiritual essence was completely absorbed.

"Oh God, don't let them see us. Quick, Sophia, help me with the body."

Sophia broke away from the feelings of pain and helped prop the body up off the road next to the storm water drain, where they wriggled under it to hide between it and the gutter, praying the corpse would restrict their light.

The demonic entities had finished devouring the soul and Sophia peered through a gap near the man's armpit, watching the swarm hover. The mass was turning, searching below, and began to unite: the winged entities were imp-like, forming, defragmenting, reforming, shapeshifting until they became one giant monster with the head of a bat, the torso of a man with leathery wings, claw feet, and a long, sharp, jagged scorpion tail. It was a giant of a beast. It dropped from the sky onto the street and the impact rumbled like thunder through the ground; the buildings shifted and windows exploded as cracks opened wide along the street and the road collapsed, creating a sinkhole.

Sophia and Father McDonald lay under the dead man's body not daring to move. Sophia held onto her necklace, her precious family heirloom, for courage. She squeezed her eyes tight and imagined being at home, when she began to feel a gentle summer breeze ruffle her favorite dress. Then she saw the wind touch the tip of the tall blades of grass; she feasted on the familiar fields and flowing river, the place she called home. She felt at peace and took a deep breath and breathed in the beauty of the day.

Father McDonald, too, felt a breeze, a gagging stench, as the beast sniffed and snorted at the dead man's body.

Sophia kept focusing on the gentle breeze in the fields and her image was getting stronger, panoramic. She felt her hair whipping across her face, the wind building around her, bursting with energy, changing to gale-force. Suddenly her hair and her clothes froze. Her state was shifting: flashing between the fields and lying under the dead body. The states merged into one existence and storm clouds from the fields appeared in the sky above the beast and lightning flared. The wind intensified. Debris went flying as a twister developed and traveled towards Sophia and Father McDonald; Sophia had become the eye of the storm. Her inner storm, which had been building up and up, exploded from her solar plexus and the two storm cells emerged and blasted the demon into a million pieces again, back into its weaker viral state. It was scattered in every direction for miles and miles. The ferocious storm lasted less than half a minute then the wind disappeared leaving a few leaves floating in its wake. Father McDonald and Sophia rolled out from under the body and staggered to their feet.

Sophia held her head, feeling groggy and unsteady. "I don't drink alcohol, except for a sip from the chalice, and I certainly never will if this is what it feels like. Maybe, if this ever ends, I can teach teenagers how to get high on light. I can start up a club." Sophia rapidly blinked, trying to clear the fog from her eyes. "Focus! What am I thinking, what was I doing?" Her vision was blurry and her ears were ringing. She waited for her blood pressure to return to normal as she harvested her energy. Father McDonald put his arm around her, to steady her on her feet. She felt the warmth of his body and looked up at his lanky frame. He was old and fragile, but nevertheless a tower of strength to her. "We have to run," she said, pulling at his arm weakly, "before they regroup and come looking for us."

The sound of a horn blasted from the alley. A four-door blue sedan sped around the corner, heading straight at them. Sophia jumped out of the way as the car braked and the tyres screeched while the car turned in an arc and came to a stop beside them.

The passenger side window rolled down and the driver leant across and shouted, "I had a dream! Get in." He looked in his rear-vision mirror. "You did all this?"

Sophia smiled at Joe. "Not all of it."

"Get in."

Without further hesitation they jumped in the car. They raced along the streets as fast as Joe dared, dodging abandoned or burnt-out cars for about five minutes until he finally slowed down. "Heck, what happened last night?"

"Thanks, Joe. What was your dream?" Sophia asked, rummaging in her backpack. She opened a paper bag and pulled out a white sage stick. She broke off a piece and handed it to Joe.

"In my dream we were cooking in your family's bed and breakfast and you were laughing and shimmying in the kitchen. The next scene was I had to get up and leave Glasgow immediately to find you both. So I did. What's this?"

"It's white sage and it will help keep you free of negative energies. If you are going to stay with us, you are going to need it for protection from the dead and the living."

"The dead?" Joe started chewing.

"We'd better tell you our story," Father McDonald said. "You need to know what you are getting into. You might recognize me if I shaved off my beard and got a haircut," Father McDonald said. "My name is Ian McDonald. I am a minister of the church and this is Sophia. Her family died years ago and she has been under my care ever since."

"No need to shave, I recognized you both. Didn't know where from. After a while I remembered watching the tube. I was about to turn it off, had my finger on the button when your wee smiling face popped on the screen. Yesterday I recognized Sophia first when she smiled. She didn't look like she was being held against her will, and you, sir, didn't come across as anything but a God-fearing man."

Sophia sat back in her seat and closed her eyes. She visualized a reflective sphere around the vehicle, a cocoon of emerald-green, purple, yellow, orange, blue and, of course, a soft touch of red for vitality — a seamless mirror. Anyone or anything that looked at them would see no more than a reflection of themselves. Good would see good, and evil would see evil.

They had been driving for a while and were entering the center of the waking city of Edinburgh. Sophia leant her head against the window, watching people with half-open eyes. They walked without purpose along the sidewalk like zombies. No hint of emotion, just moving machines, religiously following a well-worn path. There was a man with a briefcase in his hand, his eyes hidden behind black, police, frameless glasses. He reminded Sophia of some of the characters in an old classic movie, *The Invasion of the Body Snatchers*.

Joe wanted to put his foot down and hightail it out of there, but he knew it would only attract attention. He held the steering wheel tight, gripping and un-gripping. Rubbing his sweaty palms on the leg of his pants and mopping the perspiration from the side of his face onto his shoulder, he looked into the rear-vision mirror at Sophia. "Can you see if they've got the virus?"

She wondered about telling him. *Is ignorance best? Maybe not.* "Yes."

"Are there many?" Joe asked.

"They're all infected, Joe. Their souls are hanging by a thread to their body. The demonic entities can't take up a hundred per cent residence because the body will perish. A fragment of the soul is trapped, tethered to the body while it's used as the devil's puppet."

"What does it look like? Oh, my god, did you see that guy's face at the lights? It just transformed and snarled like a monster as we passed. Why aren't they attacking? Why are they still driving?"

"Robotic behavior. They can't see us, they can only see a reflection of themselves. The virus looks like a grey cloud filled with tiny metallic flies. They are passing in and out of people's noses, mouths, eyes and ears. Some latch on and hang off the body."

Father McDonald scratched the side of his head, his skin crawled. He wanted to run and dive into a body of water. He rubbed his back against the car seat feeling uncomfortable at the image conjured by Sophia's description. He pulled his Bible from his jacket pocket and prayed.

Joe ducked down a side street before realizing it was a bad idea. A few feet away he saw three men in suits attacking a woman lying next to a Vespa bike. He wanted to jump out and help. He slowed. The men stopped, as if listening, and turned towards them. Satisfied there was no one there, they leant over the woman. One man unhinged his mouth, covered the woman's bloody lips and sucked. Her cheeks collapsed. The other man pushed him aside and did the same thing. They seemed to grow taller, wider. Finished, they picked up their briefcases, and started moving closer to the car. Moving purposely towards them, running. Joe put the car in reverse and swung back out into the main street.

"Calm down, Joe, don't speed, it will be okay. They can't really see us. They're not sure what they see," Sophia said.

Father McDonald stopped praying and made eye contact with Joe. "God is with us. Just don't panic."

The stream of cars thinned out and they slowly made their way out of the city. It seemed like a lifetime to Joe. Sophia gave him a fresh piece of sage and he shoved the dried head into his mouth and chewed. He opened the window to clear the car of his stale perspiration.

"Let me drive for a while," Father McDonald said.

"No, it's okay. I need to drive," Joe said.

"That reminds me," Father McDonald said, "of when I was a kid and we were driving to the seaside, a place called Saltcoats, for a holiday and my dad ..."

Sophia tuned out, having heard the story a hundred times, and closed her eyes. "Casey, can you hear me?" she whispered in her mind, then a little louder. But there was no answer.

4

S = K LOG W: JADE. AUSTRALIA

"Where's your dad, how did you get here?" Callie asked. Kevin pushed his ear against the door trying to hear a little clearer. His dad walked up the stairs with Molly asleep in his arms.

"Psst, what are you doing?" Daniel whispered.

Startled, Kevin jolted back from the door. His face turned red. He lifted up his shoulders and dropped them.

"Get away from the door. Give them some privacy." Daniel slapped Kevin gently on the side of the head. Kevin's hair flicked up and dropped back into place. "Go downstairs and watch your brother." Daniel disappeared into Molly's room. He turned on the rotating light which cast a production of colored ponies on the walls and into the hallway.

Kevin tiptoed past the room, dodging the odd squeaky floorboard. He stopped at the first step and looked back down the hall to his mother's room. He was resisting the urge to go back and listen when his dad came out of Molly's room.

"You're not — seriously?" his dad said.

"What?"

"You know what, eavesdropping, that's what," he whispered.

Kevin pushed his hand up over his forehead, running his fingers through his hair and feeling the softness of his hair. He was frustrated he didn't know what was going on and what Jade might say. Kevin started down the stairs with Daniel on his tail. Once out of earshot of Molly's room, Daniel probed Kevin.

Daniel pulled out an assortment of ingredients for their pizzas. "Start grating," he said, handing Kevin the cheese.

"So, Kevin, what's her name? And what did you mean, you found the girl?"

Alex ran into the kitchen and pulled at Kevin's arm. Kevin shook him off, and continued grating the cheese.

"Alex, what did we say about running in the house? Go back and come in again. Without running!" Daniel said.

"Sorry, Daddy." Alex spun around and slid on his socks across the kitchen floor and out of the room, but re-entered the kitchen slowly, marching up to Kevin again. He stamped his feet and said, "Come play with me. Come on, come play with me. I'm at level five, about to fight the evil monster. Come on, it's on pause." Alex had his hands in Kevin's back pockets. He tugged and tugged. "Come on."

"Okay, okay," Kevin said, grateful that Alex was being a pest. "Dad?"

"Go on. We can talk when your mother is ready. But first, what's her name?"

"Jade." Kevin went into the living room and plonked himself on the floor next to Alex. He watched Alex battle the animated monster, but his mind was miles away.

"WHAT HAPPENED TO YOU? How do you know Kevin? I have so many questions, Jade. But you look like you need a warm shower right now," Callie said, turning on the light in her en suite.

Jade followed her into the bathroom with the pile of Kevin's clothes. Callie hung a fresh towel on the rail for her.

Jade sat on the edge of the bath and massaged her feet on the bamboo mat. Jade had had sleepless nights thinking of all the questions she would ask Callie if she ever had the opportunity. In a barely audible voice, not making eye contact, she asked, "Where did you go that night? Why didn't you come and see me? You were the last person to see my mom, and you ran." Jade pushed her hair back behind her ears and looked up at Callie. She raised her voice. "You came to our home and ate at our table. I thought you were more than just another one of my mom's post-grad charity cases. I thought you were my mom's friend, my friend, but you just left us." Jade's face contorted in anger and resentment. She stood up, grabbed her shoes and headed for the door. She stopped at the bathroom threshold and said, "Within hours of her going missing, you were on a plane, and out of the country! Where were —" Jade's throat tensed with anger and she couldn't speak. She choked on tears and confusion and she felt suffocated with emotions. The room started to spin. Jade believed that Callie knew something about her mom's disappearance. "Why won't you tell me?"

"I'm sorry, Jade, I'm so sorry. I had to think about my own family, my own life. There are people that wouldn't hesitate to hurt my family, or kill you if they thought your mother had shared her knowledge with me."

"Did she?" Jade asked.

"They would have taken me too. It has haunted me. Believe me, I regret it every day."

Jade stood still, flecks of silver light dancing behind her eyes. She no longer paid attention to what Callie was saying; she had cheated herself, allowing anger to control her. Behind her eyes, Jade's inner night sky was filled with diamonds splashing across her consciousness. She had an overwhelming sensation to just drop into infinity, endless space. Her legs and body felt heavy. Spots swam before her eyes. She knew logically what was happening, and it was controllable in her mind, but still her body was reacting, which made her even angrier. She fumbled for the edge of the bath and dropped her head into her hands.

"Jade, you okay. Just breathe. Where's your puffer?"

"I lost it."

"Wait there." Callie ran into her bedroom, and Jade could hear her opening and closing drawers before returning with a Ventolin puffer. Callie shook the puffer so it was ready if Jade needed a dose. "Relax, Jade, it's a panic attack, it will pass — breathe in slowly, 1 ... 2 ... 3. Breathe out to the count of three." Callie spoke while Jade struggled to regain her composure.

The room was blacked out. Jade couldn't see the bamboo mat under her feet, but she could still feel it and hear Callie's voice. Her body felt like it was going in slow motion. Jade focused on the feeling of her chest rising and expanding as she followed Callie's instructions.

"That's it, relax, and breathing in slowly 1, 2, 3, and out again, slowly 1, 2, 3 ... I see you found your bracelet. Your mom had me searching high and low for that. It must really be important, she was ropeable."

The darkness started to evaporate. The light of the room appeared behind her eyelids. She blinked until she was able to see and the flickers of light disappeared. Jade looked down nervously at the bracelet and twirled it around her wrist. Callie kept speaking. Jade began to relax, tracing the patterns with her fingers.

"It reminds me of a turtle shell," Callie said, watching Jade relax as she focused on the bracelet.

"It was my great-grandmother's. People called her Great Turtle. But you know that, don't you?"

"Where's your dad, Jade?"

Jade wasn't sure what she should say. She didn't want to lie because she just wasn't good at it, and she was tired, so tired. She just wanted to get clean and crawl into her bed. She didn't know what to say, or how Callie was going to react to being told that Kevin had the ability to create a hole in the universe. *Should I just say it: by the way, Kevin possesses the ability to apply the laws of quantum physics and step into a parallel universe. He has journeyed beyond reality as we know it; across time and space where he found me at the mercy of the wilderness. Somehow, I don't think she's going to warm to the idea.* "I was kidnapped and Kevin found me. I don't know what happened."

"I saw on the news that you were missing. But how did you get here, to Australia?"

It felt strange to say it, but there was nothing else that came to mind. Jade always had the answers, but this time she was lost. "I just don't know what happened."

"Are you saying ... the kidnappers, brought you here? Where's your dad?"

"At home looking for me, I guess. I don't know how I got here."

"All planes have been grounded, Jade. In every country around the world." Callie's eyebrows knotted together; confused. "But how ... perhaps the military, your mom thought her research was being monitored. They're the only planes that would get clearance to fly. But why would they bring you here? How did you escape them? And what do you mean, Kevin found you? Where did he find you?"

"Look, I'm tired, Callie, and hungry. You haven't answered any of my questions. All I can tell you is this: I was swimming on Myrtle Beach with Ben," she said, looking at Callie. If Callie was interested in the slightest about her being out with a boy, she wasn't showing it. "I surfaced, and I was hit from behind."

"Jade, that's terrible!" Callie started to check her head and found no wounds. Her beautiful black hair had clumps of coagulated blood, but no visible injury.

"Then, next thing I remember," Jade said, pulling away from Callie, "is that I woke up to the sound of men talking. It was muffled; my head was splitting and I was loaded up with narcotics. Comparatively, my ability to walk was very compromised. My neurons were cross-wired. I crumbled like a piano accordion and passed out. I woke again; I don't know how much time had passed. I was alone in a cabin on a makeshift bed, hooked up to an IV. They had taken my blood and kept me drugged up. I pulled the IV line out and after a while was able to get myself up off the bed. I suppose they thought the drugs were enough to keep me restrained, but I managed to get outside. It was daylight and I just started staggering and running and running till I passed out. I regained consciousness and started moving; it was getting dark and I passed out again. The rest is just a blur. I was lying in the woods when Kevin and Tim helped me. I regained consciousness, startled by the guys. They looked harmless enough, so I allowed them to help me up and then they brought me here. That's all my mind can recall right now. It's probably blocking stuff to protect me." Jade stared at Callie, waiting to see what she accepted.

Callie searched Jade's eyes looking for answers. It was

like a stand-off between them. Callie was unable to see beyond Jade's shattered appearance. This was a child, but it was Jade, and she wasn't an average girl. If it had been anyone else, she would not have believed her. "They took your blood, do you know why?"

"No, but logically I would have to assume there would be a connection to my mom."

"Oh, sweetie, maybe we should take you to the hospital, get you checked out. We might find a strand of hair or skin under your nails; you know that might be all it takes to track your kidnappers."

"No, that's not necessary; I don't think there would be anything of significance. I just want to be clean, I stink. I just want to wash this all away." She caught a glimpse of herself in the vanity mirror and quickly turned away.

"The hospital is packed," Callie said. "Not really a healthy place to be right now anyway. Jump in the shower and we can bag your clothes for analysis later if we need to. You feel okay, right, besides the anxiety and vertigo? You must be so tired, and your dad must be frantic. We'll call him when you're ready. Maybe Kevin can fill in some of the blanks and explain how he found you, and where he found you?"

"How long have I been missing?" Jade said, dropping the soiled jacket on the clean bathroom floor.

"Seven days," Callie said, checking the needle marks along Jade's arm. God knows what they'd put into her veins.

"Seven days? I feel like it has only been a day or two, three tops."

Callie got up from the toilet seat and made her way into the bedroom.

"Don't leave. I feel irrational. I'm afraid the world will

drop out from under me again. I know it's not real. Am I really here, Callie?"

"I won't leave," Callie said. "Yes you're really here. I'm going to sit on the edge of the bed and think."

"Okay. Keep talking, so I can hear your voice." Jade shouted over the splashing water of the shower. "Tell me about my mom's research." The water felt so refreshing. She lost herself in the rhythm of the spray massaging her body. The water turned red and swirled down the drain at her feet. She sat on the floor with the soap, and rubbed her hair until the water ran clear. Grateful for the fresh apple-smelling shampoo, she vigorously rewashed her hair before combing conditioner through with her fingers. She could no longer hear Callie. A light film of steam was building and, using her index finger, Jade drew on the wet glass: $S = k \log W$, and then a shape of a circle with a square around it. Her stomach started rumbling, snapping her out of her zoned out thinking. Jade hadn't noticed the door had been slightly closed. She strained to listen and heard Callie softly singing 'Songbird', a song Jade's mother had once loved to sing. Ever since her mother left it always made her cry. She rinsed off the conditioner and turned off the water, pulled down the towel from the rail and wrapped it around her. Quickly she dried herself and pulled on Kevin's cargoes and t-shirt. She tugged a comb through the tangles in her hair. She felt around her head for any sign of the laceration ... nothing. She shook her head in amazement at the speed of healing within the parallel world. Grabbing her hair, she twisted it into a bun at the back of her neck.

Callie was sitting on a deep-blue bedspread that had half a dozen white daisies embroidered across it. She stared at the ceiling as if something was written on it and she was trying to process its meaning. Jade stepped into the room.

The coolness of the floor reminded her of home and the last time she rose from her own bed; she had floated down the hall to the smell of burnt toast.

Callie's window was open and the nylon curtains gently flapped. A tree blocked the bigger view beyond the window, but the sound and the smell of the evening was still homely amongst all the chaos.

"Callie?" Jade looked around the room. On top of a tall, white chest of drawers, a digital picture frame was scrolling images of crystal clear waters, laughing children, memories of happier days. "Callie?"

Startled out of her own deliberations, Callie quickly turned around, looking over her shoulder, wiping away tears, and smiling. "That's better, that's the Jade I know. Who on earth were you trying to impress with those short shorts? You're a beautiful girl. It's good to see you out of black." Clenching her tissue in one hand, Callie picked up her mobile and started to call Jade's dad. Jade was taken aback that Callie had his number.

"Hi, yeah, she's out of the shower. I'll just put her on." She handed the phone to Jade. Surprised, Jade stared at the phone and then back at her. *She must have already spoken to her dad while I was in the shower.*

"Dad?"

"Thank God you're safe! I couldn't believe it when Callie called. I'm unable to imagine what you have been through."

"Dad ..."

"What happened?

"Dad ..."

"I'm sorry, you must be traumatized."

"Dad! I'm okay, confused, I don't know what happened. It's hard to believe I'm in Australia. I was at the beach —"

"What were you doing out with a boy? He claimed you

were knocked by a speedboat and dragged on board. The police thought that you had drowned and that Ben was making it up. There were no other witnesses."

"Okay — but I'm not dead." As soon as it was out of her mouth she knew it was stupid. "I think it's got to do with Mom. I really believe she is still alive, Dad."

"Honey, I'm so glad to hear your voice. I don't know how I'm going to get to you, or how to get you home."

"I can stay here with Callie. Is the old Indian still keeping watch?"

"We talked this morning. He asked me to go with him into the hills. He said he must keep me safe because we are family and you will one day return with your mother. Why did you ask about the old fellow?"

"I don't know. An image of him jumped into my mind when Callie handed me the phone. Don't go back to work, Dad. Wait until a vaccine has been developed. Go with the Indian."

"Your mother and Callie were so close. If she hadn't vanished they would have succeeded by now, I know it."

"What?" Jade let her hair out to drop over her face to hide the fresh tears. "Dad, what did the Indian say about Mom?"

"Don't worry about that, he's just hopeful."

"I need to go eat something. I don't remember the last time I ate. I am losing perspective."

"Lucky you're not driving."

"Dad, that seriously was a dysfunctional attempt at a joke."

"I love you, little Raven Wings."

Her great-grandmother named her Raven Wings when she was born. She believed Jade would be like the raven that appears when there is sickness and disaster, bearing gifts of healing upon its wings for all those who desired to be healed. The memory of Great Turtle telling her the tale over and over again was exploding inside her and she just wanted to run into her dad's arms and cry. No one had called her Raven Wings since Great Turtle's death.

"I love you too, Dad," she said, hiding her emotions.

"Call me every day, and listen to Callie. She has been the one person I have been able to talk to since your mother disappeared. She understands what we are going through."

Jade looked over at Callie, ashamed of her own previous assessment. "Okay, Dad, till tomorrow." Jade pushed the end button and handed Callie back her phone.

"You and Mom were working on the vaccine." Jade put the mobile phone down on the bedside table and said, "Why didn't you tell me?"

"I don't know what you are talking about. Let's get something to eat."

"Tell me!"

"It's not going to happen! You need to trust me when I say I don't know anything about a vaccine." Callie put her hand gently on Jade's shoulder, guiding her towards the bedroom door and out into the hallway. Arms across her chest, Jade reluctantly let Callie maneuver her. They peeked in on Molly. The yellow glow of the hall light shone through the crack and streamed across Molly's cot. Ponies were dancing across the walls, a change table sat under the window and stuffed toys filled the shelves. Baby animals hung from a mobile above the cot, swaying in a gentle breeze. Callie closed the window and Jade stepped further into the room. Molly was on her stomach with her knees curled up to her chest as if she was trying to crawl in her sleep. They both quietly left the room, closing the door.

Walking on the stairs behind Callie, Jade casually

rubbed the back of her head still expecting to feel a gash, but it was completely gone. Her legs felt heavy, but her mind was racing with questions. A quantum jump through time and space from one side of the world within minutes, involving a high level of physicality, and days had passed, not to mention the healing of her wounds once she had gone through the membrane. She started to feel rejuvenated, light, and endless possibilities flooded her mind.

WHAT ARE *they doing up there,* Kevin wondered. It was dark outside. At least an hour had passed since Jade and his mom went upstairs. Alex had stopped slaying dragons on his Xbox and had crashed on the lounge. Daniel was about to lift him up when Callie and Jade came into the living room. They both looked like they had been crying. Daniel looked at Kevin. Kevin's eyes widened and his chin tucked in, as if to say, *Don't look at me, I don't know.* Through semi-clenched lips he huffed a sigh, the air blowing his fringe. He prepared himself for a battle with his mom. He had no idea what Jade had said, but he didn't think his mom was going to like any of it. Did she tell her about the parallel world? And it was his fault that they were in there. Does she know that they were lying about being at Shaun's? He was freaking out; he was going to burst not knowing. He could see her mouth opening, she was going to speak. Fire, like with Alex's monster, was going to come out of her mouth and turn him to ash.

"Kevin," she said.

He waited, it seemed like forever; a siren went off in the night as if alerting him to the impending doom about to fall upon him. Okay, snap out of it, he told himself. *I've been hanging with Tim a little too long.* He took in a deep breath, closed his eyes and searched the space to gauge their emotional state.

"Kevin, stop it," his mother said.

He quickly opened his eyes, pretending he had momentarily drifted into sleep.

"Take Jade into the kitchen and show her how we make pizzas."

Kevin was confused. His dad saw it on his face, and said, "You're in for a treat, Jade. Kevin scatters cheese like nobody else."

Kevin smiled. *What* was his dad raving about?

"Daniel, can you help me with Alex?"

"Sure."

Kevin and Jade walked into the kitchen. Kevin scratched his head and said, "Okay, grab a pizza tray, then take what you like," indicating the prepared ingredients on the bench.

"I hope you're going to wash your hands before touching the food," she said.

He looked down at his hands and said, "Why? They're clean."

"You just scratched your head. Do you have any idea the number of germs that can be packed onto a pinhead?" Jade followed Kevin and picked up the tray: the dough was already laid out on it. Kevin leant close into her space and quietly asked, "What did you tell her? How do you know my mom?"

Jade looked down at the ingredients and scooped up a spoonful of tomato paste spreading it over her base.

"Well?" he demanded.

"Do you have any avocado?" she asked, teasing him.

"Forget the avocado. How do you know my mom and what did you tell her?"

"Who, the dragon lady? Ha ha. I told her I don't know how I got here and you and Tim found me in the bush. She'll probably ask you where exactly."

"That's it, nothing else?" he asked.

"Nothing else that involves you."

"How do you and my mom know each other?"

"She stayed with us while she was assisting my mother with genetic research. My mom was researching free radical cell mitosis, primarily a mutant cell multiples by division and destroys the organs. She believes she found a way to reverse and stop the destructive cells. Come to think of it, if that was the case, then they may have been able to ..." Jade went off into deep thoughts on how the theory could be a vaccine, for the virus.

Kevin watched her and could feel her intense emotional journey of discovery as she tilted her head to one side, her eyes squinting, circling the ceiling as if finding ideas and searching for answers. She was like an astronaut, floating into the unknown regions of space, seeking the unknown, believing something else was there, just beyond her reach. *So this is what I look like to Tim.* "Earth to Jade, Earth to Jade, come in, Jade." She looked back down at the tomato paste so he nudged her and she nearly lost her balance.

"What did you do that for?"

"You were off with the fairies. You're the missing girl! Your mom went missing and now you. But you're here. What happened, why were you in the forest? And my mom stayed with you in the US, right?"

"Yes. As soon as my mom went missing, your mom packed her bags and was off on a flight home. She left before we even got home from the police station."

Kevin reached for the mushroom and the tomato, spreading them around his pizza before smothering it with three types of cheese. Jade robotically followed his actions, shuffling along the bench. He pulled the metal handle of the oven, the heat shooting out; he instantly pulled his head back and banged into Jade's.

"Shit! That hurt," she said.

"Oh — really sorry."

Jade slid her pizza on the bottom shelf and said, "Now it's my turn to ask a question. How do you do it? How do you access a parallel world? Will you show me?"

"I don't know how I do it. I think I just slipped into it."

"If you like, I can help you work out how to do it. We can treat it like a scientific problem. That way, you will have a method to follow in the future, or a documented procedure to share with the world."

"Jade, I'm trying not to use my — gifts. It freaks out my mom."

"Why, that doesn't sound like your mom."

"I don't know what happened over there, but when she got back here, she was different and things went from bad to worse at sonic speed. My grandparents died in a car accident when coming to visit us, she quit her research and she has been fighting with my dad ... and hiding."

"What do you mean, *hiding*?"

"She doesn't let me see her emotions, unless it's her anger."

"What do you mean, see emotions? You mean facial expressions and body language?"

"No, I see them in colors around the person. I feel them in the pit of my stomach, and taste the pain in my throat. I feel your excitement right now, and I feel your confusion and sadness when you think of your mom, and your hope of finding her alive. I feel the anxiety you're always pushing away. You're afraid the room will start to spin and you will faint. You think I can help you find your mom, but I can't."

"Wow! That's incredible. That makes me feel —"

"Vulnerable and uncomfortable," he said.

"You're freaking me out." She stepped back. *Okay Jade, pull yourself together; what are the facts, let's get the facts.* "Were you always able to sense others' feelings and thoughts? Or only since you were in the parallel space?"

He could feel her deliberately regrouping and adopting a new stance. "Always," he said. "I've tried to shut it down, push it away, pretend it's not happening. Hiding away."

"Hiding — that's what you just said about your mom. You have an amazing ability to know what someone else is feeling."

Kevin and Jade were at the bench talking, their backs to the door, when Daniel cleared his throat and said, "So, you're Ellen's daughter." He held out his hand to shake hers.

Quickly Kevin jumped in and said, "Dad, I think she's got OCD. You might have to wash your hands first."

Jade elbowed Kevin in the ribs and shook Daniel's hand.

"I wish it could have been under pleasanter circumstances," Daniel said. "Callie spoke highly of your mother."

"Are we going to leave, like the policeman suggested?" Kevin asked.

"I don't think so. Where would we go?"

5

CELESTIAL WARRIORS: SOPHIA. SCOTLAND

Joe hit a bump in the road, startling Sophia from her waking dream. She blinked and pinched herself, making sure she was back in the car. She dipped her neck to the left, and then the right, to stretch it. Fields of poppies sailed past as Joe picked up speed before coming to a sudden stop. Up ahead was an abandoned military blockade.

"We're not going anywhere along this road," Joe said.

Abandoned cars led up to a tall, electric fence. Hanging off the fence were dozens of jittering bodies. How they were still alive, Sophia couldn't begin to imagine.

"Bless these souls that hang before me," Joe said.

"Amen," said Father McDonald.

Joe reversed the car, swinging it around. He turned down a side road and pulled over.

"Where are we?" Sophia asked.

"We're past Paisley, heading south-west."

"We have to be on the east coast," she said, unbuckling her seat belt and leaning her arms on the back of the front seats. The sky was a hive of activity and growing darker. The light of the sun was hidden behind the iron-colored clouds.

"We tried, we can't get through. I had to turn around. We are being pushed in this direction," Joe said.

"Then we should keep moving," Father McDonald said, "in the direction God is guiding you. You asked him to bless the souls that belonged to those bodies; he will also bless you for asking. Don't be reactive, trust in the light."

Joe twirled the red string around his wrist and counted the seven knots his brother had tied. It was starting to look a little frayed. He reached for the light switch.

"No, don't turn them on." Sophia nearly jumped over the seat to turn them off herself.

Joe felt her urgency. His skin crawled with fear. He felt himself fraying like his red string. The clouds merged together and it was hard to see the road in front of them.

"Drive," Father McDonald said, pulling off the handbrake.

"I can't." Joe was feeling melancholy and extremely tired. "No, I have to sleep now." His eyes started to close; his arms dropped from the steering wheel.

"Yes, you can!" Sophia said and pinched him at the base of his neck. Joe jumped in pain, his eyes opened and he stared with a blank face. The horror of the bodies hanging from the gate flashed in front of his face, along with his brother's body and all the images of death that the media shared: it was overwhelming.

"No, I need to sleep."

The skies grew even darker; the howling wind was rocking the car. "We have to go. If you don't we are going to die, Joe. God sent you to help us. You must push aside the lingering negative images. The demonic angels have also heard your prayers for blessings for those poor souls. They are now searching for you; they heard your tears, Joe. God believes in you and they know it."

Sophia placed her hand on the back of his neck. His mind filled with images of his mother putting his first red string around his tiny chubby wrist, the sweetness of his first kiss, his first love, and how alive he felt. He saw the memory of his brother's wedding day. He saw the images of hellos and goodbyes, and the smiles from the people who came and went from his restaurant. Sophia withdrew her hand gently; the images faded, but his feelings remained high. "Connect to those feelings, Joe."

He put the car into gear and drove blindly into the darkness.

Sophia sat back against the seat, closed her eyes and imagined a tether, like a leash to a dog, and left her body. She only went up a short distance, stopping just outside and hovering over the roof of the car. It was too dangerous to venture further, she would be noticed. She couldn't move beyond the fragile protective shell. She flipped over onto her back and looked up. Above, in the sky, angels — bad and good — battled, armed with bolts of lightning. The lights were diminishing as celestial warriors were beaten and the devil's horde absorbed their essences. There was one angel that grew brighter; it had three sets of wings and wielded a sword, its breath fire like a dragon. Its enemies were reduced to ash and the substance floated from the sky to land on the windscreen.

Joe turned on the wipers and Father McDonald prayed from Ephesians 6:10-18. "Wherefore take unto you the whole armor of God that ye may be able to withstand in the evil day, and having done all, to stand. Stand therefore, having your loins girt about with truth, and having on the breast-plate of righteousness; And your feet shod with the preparation of the gospel of peace; Above all, taking the shield of faith, wherewith ye shall be able to quench all the fiery darts of the wicked. And take the helmet of salvation, and the sword of the Spirit, which is the word of God: Praying always with all prayer and supplication in the Spirit, and watching thereunto with all perseverance and supplication for all saints."

"Amen," Joe said, and started mumbling his own prayer. "Ana beko'ach gedulat yeminecha tatir tzrua. Kabel rinat amecha sagevenu taharenu nora ..."

Joe glanced into the rear-vision mirror. Sophia's body was still and upright and tears dripped from her chin. Her spiritual body, outside, could no longer endure the visions of the battle. She was starting to feel the hand of darkness grappling for her heart and soul. She had forgotten why she came out here and slipped back into her physical body, ignoring the pain of her ethereal body retracting. Before opening her eyes or entirely merging back into herself, she said, "Take the next turn."

"Left or right?" Joe said. She didn't answer.

"You'll know it when you get there," Father McDonald said.

"I can't see shit! Sorry, Father." Up ahead, he saw a pinprick of light and wondered if it was real or just his imagination. "Can you see that?"

"See what, Joe?" Father McDonald asked.

"That light? It's growing." He thought he heard his mother calling his name from deep within his head. He watched the speck get bigger and bigger until a form appeared, with three sets of wings slowly unfolding, surrounded by divine light. "Can you see it now? It's right in front of us."

Father McDonald was in a cold sweat as he sat forward,

pressing hard against the dashboard, straining to see; his palms left damp imprints that quickly faded. "I see nothing, Joe."

He was so close Joe could see the definition in the angel's anatomy and its youthful face. Joe was afraid he was going to hit it, crash and kill them all. After driving in pitch black, the light was so blinding. He had to close his eyes. He yanked the steering wheel, turning sharply to the right, the car sliding and swerving. He corrected and opened his eyes and the sky was its usual pale grey, and the sun was shining somewhere. He slammed on the brakes.

"I told you, Joe, you would know," Sophia said.

"Can we pull over for a wee bit, hen?" Joe asks.

"That's a good idea."

"There is a tiny bit of forest about five minutes ahead. A cluster of trees of sorts. I'll pull up over there and hide the car." They went off road, squeezing between the hazel and mountain ash trees. They got out of the car and stretched their legs. Sophia was a little unsteady, but quickly came good. Father McDonald put his hands to his lower back and stretched backwards, cracking arthritic bones, while Joe stretched his arms up and down. They looked like a bunch of friends limbering up to do calisthenics. Under any other circumstance it would be funny.

"I think I know this place, it's a wooded glen. We're near Dusk Water, not far from the coast," Joe said. "When my brother and I were young lads we used to imagine we were smugglers; our ship anchored off the coast, we would row ashore to find a hiding place for our loot, which would be Cleeves Cove caves. There are a couple of entrances to a natural cave system that has been the location of a few myths." Joe started walking off, exploring the area.

Sophia followed him, Father McDonald trailing behind

both of them with his hands on his hips, occasionally stopping to take in deep breaths of fresh air. Further into the woods, they heard a waterfall and the terrain became very damp and mossy. It was also very lovely. Sophia helped Father McDonald while he jumped over green rocks and climbed over fallen, velvety trees. Wild foliage and large trees like hazel and mountain ash. A large rock loomed above the cave's opening.

"This is awesome," Joe said. "This is the place where my childhood ghost stories began. Who figured I'd be taking refuge here one day?" He helped Father McDonald up into the entrance of the cave where he sat down to rest, clutching his chest.

"What's wrong?" Sophia crouched beside him and wrapped her arm around him.

"I need my backpack, my heart pills."

"I'll go." Joe rushed off. He swiftly jumped down over the trees and rocks and up the other side of the glen. In a short time, he was back with three backpacks.

"There in the side pocket," Father McDonald said.

Sophia fished them out and gave him the bottle. His hand was trembling, and he couldn't get the lid off. Sophia took the bottle from him and pushed a pill into the palm of his hand. He swallowed; they all waited. His color started to return and he said, "Just a few months ago, I carried you into the church and laid you down on the very pew you were born on, and today I can hardly lift up my own arm. I have aged a hundred years over the last few weeks."

"You'll be right, old man," Joe said patting him on the back. "You just need to catch your breath, and let those pills work their magic." Joe waited till Father McDonald stopped sweating and his body had relaxed.

Sophia was wiping his brow with the sleeve of her jacket. "How's the pain?" she asked.

"Just about gone, and so are my pills," he said.

"I'm going to have a wee stickybeak inside the cave, if you two are okay with that?" Joe said.

Father McDonald opened his eyes and nodded his approval and closed them again.

Joe pulled out his torch. "I won't be gone very long. Will you both be alright?"

"We'll be fine," Sophia said.

"There's some chocolate fudge protein bars in the front pocket of my pack. Help yourself." Joe walked into the limestone cave, leaving Sophia and Father McDonald to rest for a while.

The cave was cold and smelt damp. It opened up into a larger musty chamber. The further he penetrated, the more the air became stagnant. Joe took one of the tunnels branching off the main chamber that led east, further away from the coast. This is what he imagined as a kid. He stopped to lay his hand on the rock face, feeling for its heartbeat. There were more passageways branching to the left and right, but he went straight ahead, then took the second left for twenty-five yards. It started to curve and the air became sour, his eyes watering. He covered his mouth, and imagined a gutted animal that had come in to die. A real exploration of the caves would have to wait for another time, when his brother could be with him. Then he remembered the blood on the kitchen floor. His brother was dead. Lots of people were dead, and more people were going to die. He was on borrowed time; there was no later.

All of a sudden he felt claustrophobic. He had only been gone about ten minutes but it felt like an hour. He started to make his way back to the main entrance. He stopped at a junction and now couldn't recall if he had gone left or right. He stood looking down each tunnel trying to decide which way to go. Making choices wasn't his strongest trait: there were always too many variables, too many choices to weigh, so his brother, a man of action, had usually taken care of the decisions while he Joe did the hard yakka. He chose the passage on the left, but it soon became colder and unfamiliar. Joe quickly turned around and went back the way he came, moving towards the right. He arrived back at the same point and without hesitation took the right passage, and it wasn't long till he could see it opening onto the main chamber. He could see the light from outside and the silhouette of Father McDonald leaning against the cave wall, and Sophia standing at the opening tossing something into the scrub. Sophia turned towards him and he couldn't see her face; she had a glow about her. "I thought you had gotten lost." she said. "Father McDonald was exhausted so he's drifted into a deep sleep."

Joe sat down beside them and pulled out a peppermint chocolate protein bar from his backpack. He tried to rip it open, rustling the wrapper and making a considerable amount of noise. His big hands were searching for a good place to pinch the sides and pull it open, with no luck. He smacked it down on his knee hard and the bar popped out the other end. "Do you want a bite?" He offered the bar to Sophia.

"No, I'm good," she said. "I've just been enjoying an apple. I hope you don't mind?"

"No, not at all." He nodded towards Father McDonald. "Is he okay?"

"I hope so." She sat down next to the priest and wrapped her arms around her legs, resting her chin on her knees. Joe sat against the opposite wall of the entrance, and waited with Sophia for Father McDonald to wake.

"TELL me again about your red string," Sophia said.

She watched Joe look down at his wrist and start running his finger underneath it. She copied him, twirling the knots between her fingers; it was soft and she found the motion relaxing.

"It was wound around the tomb of Rachel, the matriarch," Joe said, "for her protection and blessings. For me, it is a reminder to treat people how I would like to be treated. Not to bully or judge. To forget about jealousy, because it's poisonous and makes you old and bitter. It keeps me positive. We all have negativity, we all need to duck and weave from the evil glances of others. It's also a constant reminder of my mother, my childhood, and how important it is to try and see the good in the chaos around us, especially in times like these."

Sophia watched his face change with each thought. He actually believed in what he was saying, she realized. The energy around him changed: he had started with bright vibrant shades of earthy colors and now they were softening, becoming cool blue and violet. The dominant color in the central part of his being was a glowing green. It moved like a turning crystal in the sunlight. She wondered what it would be like if what he said was true. She fiddled with her red string and wished it would come true. All the dark angels would starve and flee; they would choke and burn in hell because of the mass consciousness sending out good thoughts and desires. The world would light up like a Christmas tree every day. *Could it be that simple?*

"What you have to do is have certainty," Joe said.

"Certainty in what?" she asked.

"In whatever it is you're doing. Like how you said I would know which way to turn, back there. You had certainty; you didn't doubt it for a minute, did you?"

"Well, no."

"That's what you have to feel. That feeling where there is no possibility for anything else, no room for doubt. You have to have certainty and go for it. I had doubt and glimpsed your reflection in the rear-vision mirror. You were struggling internally and at that moment I had certainty in you."

"They should teach us this at school," Sophia said.

"Something is guiding you beyond my vision. There's something that surrounds you, a magic that floats just out of my sight, Sophia."

She saw his energy change and his muscles tense.

The sound of a couple of larrikins screeching and laughing across the paddocks could be heard through the forest canopy. Joe stopped. "They must have seen the car."

Sophia could hear the slamming of doors and the jabber about who might own the vehicle, and where they were. A dark cloud hung above them, masked by the trees but Sophia could sense it. She woke Father McDonald. "We have to go."

Father McDonald was dazed, unsure of where he was. Joe was suddenly by his side, supporting him and picking up his pack, tossing it over his shoulder and his own bag over the other.

Sophia could hear the sounds of the hooligans getting closer. "We have to go."

Father McDonald's face looked worn and old and her heart was breaking; this was too much for him. She held back her tears as she flung her backpack over her shoulder.

She had forgotten how heavy it was. She locked her arm with Father McDonald's and Joe supported him on the other side. They hung onto him while he took a moment to balance himself. His Bible fell out of his pocket. He pointed at it and Joe gracefully — for a big fellow — scooped it up and put it inside Father McDonald's coat pocket for him. Sophia was worried. The only place to hide was inside the caves.

Joe took the lead, remembering the turns he made the first time he was there. They could hear the sound of the gang entering the caves behind them.

They yelled, "Here we come, ready or not," and laughed.

Sophia turned, faced the last passageway, and focused on blocking the entrance by unfolding her energy. She felt it traveling around her body from the center of her being, down her shoulders —like sand running down her arms — and into her hands. She projected the energy outwards until it touched the walls and ceiling, creating a mirror image of the cave wall.

Sophia, Joe and Father McDonald walked deeper into the caves, then stopped to listen. They heard the fading sounds of yelling and laughing. Sophia, holding onto Father McDonald's arm, wondered who was guiding whom. She didn't know any more, but she had to protect him. He was the only one left who knew her family; *he* was her family. Sophia missed Mother Catherine and she wanted to cry remembering all she had lost in such a short time. She felt angry at God for taking her friends and family, she was angry for the pain and suffering Father McDonald was going through. She had never dared before to be mad at God. She lifted her left hand up to push strands of hair behind her ears and wiped at her eyes, and noticed the red string on her wrist. Suddenly she felt old, as if she had been fighting a battle that spanned many lifetimes, and she felt that the image she treasured of running through the streets with other kids on a hot summer's day was a mirage, an illusion. Sophia hadn't realized she was still fixed to the one spot and that they were both shining their torches at her.

"Sophia, what ya doing? We have to keep moving, hen."

Father McDonald turned off his torch and placed it in his pocket. He looped his arm tighter around hers and patted her hand. He started to tell her favorite story.

"On a fresh Saturday afternoon," he began, "before the end of autumn, amongst the fallen leaves, beside the lake, your mom and dad laid down a checked red and blue rug. Your sisters set out the contents of a picnic basket; they were all excited, and you stood a few steps back from the blanket, just out of their reach, taking off your diaper and clothes. You were wriggling out of your diaper when your sisters, who were supposed to be keeping an eye on you, noticed you had stripped. They yelled at you to stop. Sure enough as soon as everyone was watching, you started to run butt-naked across the fields, laughing. I was fishing one last time before the lake froze for the winter, and had a bird's-eye view of your devilish behavior. You were hysterical with laughter. Your sisters gave chase and you ducked down, hiding in the long green grass. You burrowed under the fallen leaves, waiting for your sisters. You popped up with splayed fingers in front of your face and roared like a lion. Quickly, you ducked back down and covered your eyes with your tiny hands, thinking no one could see you. Your sisters hid in the grass around you and when you jumped up you couldn't see them, so when they sprang up from the tall grass you fell over backwards in fright. You started crying and they were laughing; you slowly stopped crying and started laughing a little too. Your big sister scooped you up in her arms and carried you back to the rug."

Sophia couldn't help visualizing the images even though she had no memory of that day, but he had told her the story so many times, it was easy to see it in her mind's eye. She suddenly realized she had lost track of time listening to the tale as well as her sense of direction, it seemed. She searched back along the tunnels in her mind and waited. The young hooligans were lost and had given up their pursuit.

"We should go back now," Joe said.

"No," Father McDonald said, "we have to keep going."

"We can't, we don't know where we are going." Joe's voice was filled with panic. "We'll end up dying down here."

"I had a dream, a terrible dream," said Father McDonald.

Sophia looked at both men and wondered why adults freaked out so much. "We have to keep walking and you are to guide us, Joe," she said.

"This is suicide," he replied.

Sophia watched Father McDonald walk up close to Joe. She tried to peek inside Father McDonald's mind, inside his unique room, to quickly search in his grand old library amongst the polished shelves for the dream he had mentioned. But it was locked and she could only see a hard-wood door with a shiny new lock. She felt suddenly ashamed and pulled out, but not soon enough. He turned towards her as if sensing what she was doing. He frowned with disapproval; she looked away, avoiding eye contact, but sensed he was also pleased that she was still practicing using her gifts. She looked back, watching the two men and wondered if she should have a peek inside Joe's head. She pushed the thought away as quickly as it had come. She trusted Father McDonald, and even though he seemed to have aged terribly, he was strong mentally and spiritually. He showed little fear and there was no doubt in his eyes. She had followed him this far and he had protected her.

"We should turn off our torches, save the batteries," she said. "That will give us a few days with light so we don't end up in total darkness all the time."

Joe looked at her and back at Father McDonald. "A few days?"

"No doubt," she said. He was such a big cuddly bear she just wanted to wrap her arms around him.

"Oh God, what have I gotten myself into?" He looked up at the dark blank roof of the cave and back at her. "You're special, I'll give you that, but hen, you're mighty cheeky." Sophia watched him turn to Father McDonald to say, "If death wasn't walking the streets, I wouldn't stay, I have to tell you, I would hightail it out of here. We're not prepared for a hike through these caves."

"We're prepared enough, the best we could ever be," Father McDonald said.

Sophia fumbled with her torch and Joe caught her smile before she found the off button. "We love you, Joe," she said.

"Remind me never to play cards with you," he replied.

They had to take a minute for their eyes to adjust to the light of one torch; darkness suddenly seemed a little closer.

"How am I supposed to know which way to go? Shit!"

Sophia couldn't see much and stayed close to Father McDonald. They continued walking, the air cooling the deeper into the tunnels they went, turning down different passageways. It seemed hours had passed when Father McDonald stopped reciting from the scriptures and suggested they take a rest. They crouched by the wall shining the torch at the roof and shared protein bars and some water. Joe kept checking his watch, afraid he would lose track of time.

"It's still daylight," Joe said, aiming the torch at his watch, "but down here I suppose it doesn't matter. I wonder what the stars would be like tonight. I can just imagine them now."

Sophia watched him tilt his head up as if he had a sweeping view of the sky. This was their second day travelling south-east through the musty caverns. They were exhausted and covered in sweat. The rations Joe had brought were ample: the protein bars were chocolate, mint, cherry and orange flavors, but they were now running out of water.

Sophia was wondering how they were going to get to Israel. She wondered about Kevin and Jade and how they were going to meet. Sophia didn't have the answers; no pictures flashed across her mind, except for images of flames and everything burning; a wall of scorching heat. She closed her eyes and started to fall into a dreamless sleep when she unexpectedly jolted awake as a chill raced up her spine and instantly she was worried for Casey.

6

DOORMAN FOR DEATH: SHAUN.
AUSTRALIA

S haun sat on the roof, dangling his legs over the gutter, and watched the flashing police lights leave Kevin's place, only to stop in the next street. It had been days since he had seen the two retards disappear into thin air. He had waited for them to reappear after those other jerks had killed that poor German Shepherd dog. He was surprised to find he had slept through the night in the bush and had missed any reappearance of Kevin and Tim. His cheek had been throbbing so he had left his hiding spot and headed home for the comfort of his own bed and a couple of painkillers. He wasn't anxious about them; they were complete losers, but he couldn't help being curious. He was surprised to see them a little while ago walking down the middle of the street with the barefoot girl. Where had they been and who was she? Mostly he wondered, *Why do I care?* People were just disappearing, and he wished his dad would disappear. He could hear him inside the house and could smell his cigarette smoke.

"Shaun, is that you up there? Come here, I want to show you something."

Shaun looked over the side, thinking about climbing down and hightailing it out of there, but he didn't feel like wandering the streets tonight, or riding the trains. He looked over his shoulder at the solid mass of cloud boiling up over the horizon; it moved like a flock of birds rising up from the ocean and migrating towards the city. He climbed down off the roof back through the attic. His dad was standing at the bottom of the stairs holding an old photo album.

"Have you seen this picture of your mother? She's just your age."

Shaun cautiously went down the stairs looking for a hidden agenda. His dad was drunk as usual, but his words weren't as slurred. "No, I haven't," he said.

"Well, come on, boy, why you walking so slow? Take a look." He sat on the bottom step and moved across for his son to sit beside him. "Look how happy she is."

Shaun was afraid to move and he worried about his choice of words, in case they were taken the wrong way. He scratched his groin and rubbed his eyes. "She looks pleased." She was at the beach and had star-jumped off a grassy embankment; she was in mid-air, her toes pointing down towards the white sand.

"This was the first time we met," his dad said. "I was on holidays from university, and had just got back from an archaeology field trip to Peru. The last thing I wanted to see was more sand. My friend dragged me along saying it would be good for me. He was right. I met your mother, and she was the best thing in my life. I took the photo on an old instant camera, and we shook it to help it dry. I told her about Peru and she said she wanted to see the Nazca Lines." He turned the picture over and written in her handwriting was her name and phone number, with a smiley face drawn inside a flower. "I called her that very night."

His dad flicked through the album, stopping occasionally. Shaun was thinking his dad had forgotten that he was there beside him. They both looked down at his mother's ruby complexion; she was exaggerating her baby bump and laughing. His father had stopped talking. Emotions had got the better of them both. Shaun used his shoulder to casually wipe his eye, stretching, pretending he was tired. His dad slammed the album closed, and rubbed his chin before picking up the bottle by his feet and taking a long drink. He rocked a little on his heels and walked away.

Shaun sat on the step, contemplating his options. He could go to his room and lock the door before his dad started turning from a sad drunk to a violent drunk, although a locked door hadn't stopped him in the past. He moved the pouch in his pocket and could feel the different shapes of the stones digging into his thigh. He stood and put his hand in his pocket, felt the stones, and decided to go out. He had a shower and went into his room to dress in jeans and t-shirt and grabbed a lightweight hoodie. He went back into the bathroom to fish the pouch of touchstones from his dirty pants. His dad was still in the lounge room, sitting in his mother's recliner. During her last few days at home she had slept sitting up in it, because she had been unable to lie down comfortably. It was looking old and tattered, but his dad wouldn't give it up. He never washed it and believed it still smelt like her. But it didn't; it smelt of smoke and alcohol. His dad's wallet was sitting on the side table next to an empty bottle.

"You want another drink?"

His dad lifted his finger and wagged it knowingly, slowly nodding his approval. Shaun picked up the empty bottle and with a little sleight of hand scooped up the wallet. He threw the empty bottle into the trash and plucked the plastic cards from the wallet. He chose a bottle of wine from the rack, then skillfully put the bottle and wallet back on the side table and pocketed the cigarettes.

"Get a glass and I'll give you a drop."

"No, I'm good."

"You think? Too good to drink with your old man? I doubt that. Ever since you were conceived, death follows you. You're nothing but a doorman for death. You could start a euthanasia business, you wouldn't have any costs, but you're so ignorant you probably don't even know what the word means. I've heard you screaming out your little girl-friend's name at night. *Rachel, Rachel.* I should have left you there to be buried in the explosion with her."

It all came back and hit him like a giant wave. He was looking over the back seat of the Jeep, they were moving away from the caves and the mountains heading towards the Judean Desert. She stood in front of the cave as the charges his dad had laid exploded behind her. Rachel, he thought, Rachel. He couldn't feel his legs, he couldn't feel his body; his mind assaulted him with forgotten images. The drugged flight, his mother lying in hospital not getting any better like his dad had promised. He remembered whispering in her ear, telling her what his dad had done, and when she was an angel she had to look after Rachel. Shaun wanted to explode with anger, he wanted to cry, he wanted to run, but he was stuck with his father's smirking face.

"Don't tell me you had forgotten about your little girl-friend? You're useless. You can't be my son. You don't have an ounce of my brains or balls."

Shaun's fists clenched, then opened and closed again. He screamed like a wounded animal. "You're a murderer; you're not my father. You're a failure. Mom must be in hell. Fuck you, you son of a bitch. Even in heaven she would be in pain, seeing what you have become. I told her what you did. She never would have stayed with you, never." The bottle of wine beside his dad came hurtling towards him. Shaun ducked; it smashed into the wall and the LED screen.

"You're pathetic. Who the hell do you see every time you look in the mirror? Piss off, retard," his dad said.

Overwhelmed by his memories, Shaun didn't have to be told twice. He took off, slamming the front door behind him. He went to the nearest auto-teller machine, swiped his dad's card, punched in the PIN, withdrew five hundred dollars cash and headed for the train station. He couldn't get the images out of his mind. Feelings he didn't even know existed were coursing through his veins. He stepped onto the platform where a cold, sharp southerly wind blew.

Shaun felt a little spooked. The platform was deserted and vomit had dried and crusted on the only seat. There was one train scheduled to arrive in seven minutes. He walked to the end of the platform and leant his back against the brick wall. He felt for the cigarettes in his top pocket, pulled out the lighter and tapped out a smoke. He worked the lighter, then stared at the flame. The veins in his neck bulged as he screamed into the night. He slid down the wall and cried for the first time since his mother died. He thought he heard someone walking along the platform, so he wiped his eyes, spat in front of him and turned to look but there was no one else around. He lit his smoke, inhaled deeply and coughed up his guts. As soon as he stopped, he inhaled again. He drew on the cigarette as if he was drawing in the breath of life. He looked down at his hands, thinking that they were dirty; with the smoke dangling from his lips, he started rubbing them against his pants. He tossed the cigarette butt, and watched the red tip glow upon the tracks. The arriving train lights could be seen approaching the station. Shaun kept looking at the butt, wondering if he had time to jump, jump down and stamp on it, time — but it didn't matter really if he had time. It would be quick like the explosion, quick like it was for Rachel. He stepped forward over the yellow security line, everything was in slow motion. The train hurried forward sucking him towards it; the train slowed, losing its hold. It came to a complete stop. The doors opened right in front of him.

No one was in the annex stepping off so he stepped aboard, grabbing hold of the cold metal pole. It was covered with smudged handprints and gum, and he recoiled in disgust. He screwed up his nose and eyes and held his breath. A bum was camped out on the lower deck, and the stale air and the aroma of fresh urine assaulted his senses. Whoosh. The automatic doors sealed behind him. The train screeched, labored, then jerked twice as it pulled away from the station. The train rocked, picking up speed and he maneuvered towards the connecting carriage door. He couldn't believe his karma. His dad was pulling him way down, emotionally he was beginning to unravel, and when he wrenched at the connecting door lever, he found the door was locked. He let his head drop and bang hard against the window. He pushed off the door and walked through the top carriage to the other side, and this time the door was unlocked.

A nervous, fat greasy-looking man, wearing a suit with runners, clutched a briefcase in his lap. He was watching Shaun's every movement through the reflection in the window. *At least he doesn't smell, and it's better than being alone.* Shaun ignored him, walked to the back of the carriage and stretched his legs up onto the seat. He pulled his hoodie over his eyes, folded his arms across his chest and slouched down. He drifted into a restless sleep, dreaming of flying demonic angels and fire. He felt a soft whisper behind him and woke in a sweat. The train had jerked him awake as it stopped and started at a station. He read the station's name off a bench; he was a few stops away from the city. He wiped the sweat off his face with his sleeve, and closed his eyes.

The sound of the rushing wind alerted Shaun to the fact someone had just come through the connecting doors. He kept low, his eyes closed, listening to a group of teenagers walking in the lower carriage. There was a loud bang. It sounded like something or someone hitting at the windows. The noise stopped. Shaun looked up and could see the fat guy in his seat up ahead and that his shoulders and head were shaking. He then heard the first footfall on the steps leading up to the top level. The train came to the next station, the signs and building flashing past. The train didn't stop. There were three hooded guys coming up the stairs and one was banging a metal baseball bat on the rail.

"Well, looky here," the guy with the bat said, pointing it at the fat man.

Shaun kept low, knowing what these guys were capable of doing. Their tormenting and teasing had begun. The big guy was scared out of his mind. They pulled his briefcase off his lap, rummaged through the contents and tossed it about the train. Shaun heard them slap the guy on the side of his head. Yelled at him to cough up and dig into his back pocket, and hand over his wallet. Shaun had treated others the same. He knew the fat guy would be pissing himself in shock. He moved slowly, fearfully, and then the guy with the bat laid it down onto the man's shaking shoulder. He gripped the bat with both hands and yelled, "Home run!" The window became painted abstract red. Shaun kept low, avoiding being seen; he rolled off the seat and onto the floor, listening.

The assailants pulled off the guy's watch and Nikes. They dug into his pockets, pulling out his phone. Shaun kept as quiet as possible. The gang started to turn, leaving the way they had come. Shaun panicked as his mobile start to vibrate.

The train was pulling into Kings Cross station. Shaun was ready to leap out of hiding and throw himself down the stairs and out the door. He could see their feet heading towards him. His phone had stopped. They kept coming. They were talking amongst themselves.

"Try him again," one of them said.

Everything seemed to be muffled and in slow motion. Shaun held his breath; they had stopped halfway down the stairs and the last guy was swinging on the rails inches away from Shaun's head. The train jerked to a stop and they jumped down and off, onto the platform. He still couldn't see them, but he waited till the last minute before jumping up and off the train. He pulled his hood up, dug his hands into his pocket and headed in what he thought was the opposite direction. He hid amongst the few people waiting to get on the train when he thought he heard his name being called. He ignored it and kept walking, picking up his pace. He didn't understand what had gotten into him and why he was afraid of his own shadow. The world had become crazier than he was. His phone started to vibrate; he pulled it out of his pocket to see it was his mate Kyle. "Where the fuck have you been?" he said into the phone.

"Where you at, man?" Kyle said.

"Just got into the city."

"Same, dude."

"Stop shouting into the phone, you asshole." Then

Shaun realized he could hear his name being called from somewhere behind him. The three hooded silhouettes were coming towards him; the guys from the train. One had his hands dug into his pockets. *This is it*, Shaun thought, *some dude coming for revenge*. As he watched, the guy removed his hand from his pocket and he saw the shape of a gun.

"Look what we found." It was his mate, Kyle, shouting and waving the gun above his head.

Commuters kept their heads down, getting on the train and out of sight. Shaun looked at his phone and pushed "end". His friends looked and acted differently from usual. They were more violent than he could remember, and it had only been a week at most. Or had he become weak.

"Hey, mate, where have you been?" Kyle said.

"Around. Had an awesome fist-fight in the city last week, had to spend a few hours in hospital. The other dude was pretty fucked. You should have been there, man."

"Yeah, what you score?"

Shaun reached into his pocket and pulled out the wad of money he had taken out of his dad's account and waved it in the air.

"Alright, Let's party," Kyle said.

"Who's that?" Shaun asked, nodding towards the third guy.

"That's Homer."

Shaun didn't recognize the guy at first. He wasn't wearing his school baseball jacket, which he practically wore everywhere as a status symbol. *He's the state's star baseball player, headed for the big league in the US. Shit, he's even dating the retard's sister.*

Kyle chattered on. "He's got the virus and has come over to the dark side, and I think he likes it. He has one hell of a swing, man, and has found swinging at things other than balls to be more fun." As if on cue, Homer picked up the bat and swung at the ticket booth and started to beat the shit out of it. Kyle and his offsider started cheering him on and laughing as he became more enraged with each swing. Shaun started walking.

"Hey, wait up," Kyle yelled.

They followed Shaun like a pack of wild pit bull dogs, attacking and frightening people randomly.

The flashing neon lights of the city looked different, they no longer seemed real to Shaun. The menacing and minor crimes — like smashing some geek's headlights so he can't drive home, or getting drunk and picking fights, the things he generally saw and liked to do — were somehow different: there was no order to the crime he was seeing. There were guys smoking ice on the street and the little discretion prostitutes may have had was gone. There was a sense of something forbidding. Shaun felt sick. The image of a burning lion deep within a cave haunted him, waiting to drag him to hell. Relieved, Shaun saw there was no bouncer on the door of Frankie's Laboratory and they walked straight into the bar. Fluorescent lights strobed the wall and the DJ was kicking ass. The waitresses came over with a tray of syringes and injected shots of mixed alcohol into their open mouths.

Shaun's head soon started to spin and he needed fresh air, so he got up and went outside, with Kyle and the others following him. *Why do they keep following?* he wondered, and accidentally bumped into a hooker. He stepped back, nearly apologizing, but blurted out, "What the fuck! Move your skanky ass."

Kyle walked up to the woman and stuck his face into her breast and asked how much for her to get on her knees. "Pay the lady," he said to Shaun, not waiting for her to reply.

Shaun didn't recognize these guys. They've become hard-core.

They're not just a bunch of idiot teenagers any more. I need to get home.

"Yeah, great idea, Kyle. What about you two?" Shaun said. "Are up for a blow job? My shout."

"Shit, yeah," Homer said.

Shaun pulled out a couple of hundred and stuffed it between her breasts. She led them into the alley and Shaun lit a smoke.

"You're not coming," Kyle said.

"I'll join in after I have this smoke." Shaun dragged on his cigarette and waited till they were deep in the shadows. He turned the corner and walked away. He threw his butt into the gutter and crossed the road, slipped into an alley on the other side and waited. A pack of drunken girls walked past him and he pushed himself into the wall. They were tormenting an old guy who had become too friendly. They pushed him to the ground and started kicking him while people just walked on by. The virus had taken over the city. Shaun realized he had created enough negativity to fester in his aura to be able to hide in the darkness. He saw his mates come out of the shadows, looking up and down the road. They were crossing the road, heading in his direction.

They stopped to watch the girls beating the guy. Amused, Kyle said, "Let me help you, ladies," and pulled out the gun. He had a crazed look on his face and his eyes were blacker than the night. Kyle lowered the gun into the old man's face. The man held up his hands, begging for his life. Kyle fired. The girls cheered and welcomed him and his mate into their fold. They walked off, slinking into the nearest bar together.

Shaun waited for the prostitute who had given his mates a blow job to come out of the shadows, but she never did. He started to make his way back to the station, then a loud explosion lit up the streets. People ran towards the sound, excited. He kept moving through the back streets, keeping just inside the shadows. A fire truck pulled up in front of a burning skyscraper and Shaun couldn't help being entranced by the flames. People started pushing the firemen out of the way, wanting the building to burn. The spectators soon became violent, yanking the hoses from them. One police car showed up. The officers had no chance of getting out of the vehicle, because the crowd descended upon them and began rocking the car, flipping it onto its back. Then someone hurled a petrol bomb. The firefighters hosed the people away from the police vehicle and dragged the cops to safety. The crowd booed. Windows on the upper levels of the skyscraper exploded, and people were drawn to look up and cheer as shards of glass pelted down. Shaun saw that the police and firemen were searching for a place to hide and were heading in his direction. Stepping backwards down the laneway, watching the chaos, he managed to trip over his own feet. *Stuff this,* he thought, and started running to the train station.

There was one train waiting at the platform, so he ran at the security wire cyclone fence, jumped up, climbed over it, and bolted to the train. The carriage he entered was empty. He stared through the window as the train pulled out of the station. Red and orange flames licked the walls of the tall buildings. Shaun's thirst for fire had been quenched, perhaps gone forever. In that moment, watching the city burn, he felt no desire, he felt lost. The city that held happy memories of his mother was burning.

THE WINE WAS DRIPPING down the wall when he realized

Shaun had stolen his cigarettes. He slowly pushed himself out of the recliner and went into the kitchen for another pack and another bottle of wine. Before plugging in the old fan, he used his shirt to wipe away the red wine from around the socket. He liked the feeling of the breeze on his skin as he dropped back into the recliner. He uncorked the bottle of wine, took a long drink, then opened the packet of smokes. He cupped his hands around the lighter's flame, protecting it from the fan, and dragged deeply on the cigarette before sitting back and slowly blowing out the smoke. His wrist dropped onto the armrest, the cigarette dangling between his fingers, as he smiled at the wedding picture hanging on the wall behind the fan: his beautiful wife, her beautiful smile. He closed his eyes, capturing the image. The smoke continued to burn and slipped from his fingers, falling as he was sinking into a deep sleep.

The old fan shuddered back and forth over the smoldering cigarette and his slumbering body. The wine trailed down from behind the picture and over the edge of the power point into the sockets. A blue spark flared and ran up the cable into the fan's motor. It ignited into flames which instantly enveloped the nylon curtains.

JADE AND KEVIN were in the warm kitchen, gazing every few seconds through the thick glass door at their pizza. Callie, having put Alex to bed, walked in behind his dad.

"I think you have some explaining to do," she said.

Kevin felt like a trapped mouse not knowing which way to turn. He looked at Jade and recalled what she had said. *She's just going to ask you where and how you found me.* "About what?" he said, trying to act in control in front of Jade.

"Really, you're going to play that game. About what? You're kidding, right? You have been gone for three days, not three hours. That's seventy-two hours, Kevin! And you come home with a young kidnapped girl who lives on the other side of the world. And you have the audacity, to say *about what*?"

Kevin's face grew hotter with each word she spoke. He looked at his dad and he looked just as angry as she was. He hoped his voice wouldn't quiver as he answered. "Tim ... Tim and I were down at the river. We found her lying there, in the bush. She looked like she was dead. We went over to see if she was, and she opened her eyes. We helped her up, then a rabid-looking dog tried to attack us, and we ran. I told Jade you guys would help her get home. I didn't know who she was or where she was from."

"Where was Shaun?" his dad asked.

"This was after we left his place," Kevin said.

"Come on, I want you to show us," his mom said.

"Let them eat first, Cal."

"Make it quick."

"What's the rush, Cal? They can show us in the morning. We won't see much in the dark anyway."

She picked up the phone, ignoring him. Kevin tried to listen to his mom on the phone while he pulled the pizzas out of the oven, but he couldn't catch what she was saying. They ate the hot pizza straight off the tray. They only had time to eat four pieces before there was a knock at the door. Kevin jumped up, but his mother blocked him and walked to the door herself. "You finish up," she said, and opened the door. "Thanks for coming back."

Kevin thought it was the cops and he didn't want to lie to the cops. *They're going to see straight through me.* "He's in the kitchen," she said.

He wiped his mouth with the back of his hands and then slid his hands down his pants into his pockets. His shoulders slumped and relaxed as Tim walked in with his mom and sister.

"What gives, K?" Tim said, taking a slice of his pizza.

"Don't know."

"Yes, you do, you always do."

"Shh, not now," Kevin said.

"Molly and Alex are upstairs sleeping. Alex is on the recliner in Molly's room. Kath and Jade can sleep in Alex's room across from Kevin's. Molly's generally a good sleeper, although lately she has been a bit restless. You will just have to check on Alex once or twice."

Kevin watched his mom give instructions to Tim's mom and when she took a breath his dad dared to interrupt.

"The kids will be fine. They're sound asleep."

She glanced at his dad and continued speaking to Tim's mom. "Did Kath bring some clothes for Jade? And the boys can sleep in Kevin's room when we get back and you should take the guest room." Callie looked at Kevin. "Put your shoes on."

Tim followed. "Where are we going?"

"She wants to see where we found Jade."

"She knows."

"All she knows is we found her in the bush. We thought she was dead, and we helped her up and brought her here."

KEVIN WAITED for his dad to get the car out of the garage. The night was thick with smoke and he could see a glow over the city. His mom jumped in the front seat with a large dolphin torch while Tim and Jade climbed in the back with him.

Kevin took them the long way round. They weren't going to be able to drive through the vacant lot to the other side. Daniel put the lights on high beam as they came to a trail leading into the bush. They saw a dead dog lying by the road.

"Was that the dog you were talking about?" his mother asked.

"I don't know. It's hard to tell." He didn't want to look at the poor dog and it seemed everyone else felt the same, except his mom. She pulled a pair of latex gloves out of the glove compartment and jumped out of the truck to examine the carcass.

"Bullet," she said to Daniel.

They all got out of the car and circled the dog.

"Which way? Kevin, Tim, which way?" Callie asked.

Kevin saw the determination in her face and started to sense her urgency. Her guard was coming down and she was afraid, looking for something. She was desperate, hoping to find it, but outwardly showed a mask of authority. Kevin was starting to sense her true feelings and she threw a look at him, as if she felt him rummaging around inside her emotions.

He looked down and said, "This way." They came to the anthill. "We would normally have to run together over it," he said and looked at Tim. Tim looked like he was having the time of his life; just another big adventure. Jade was quiet and hanging back, but he kept an eye on her. The river was close and they could hear movements in the bush, the nocturnal animals returning to the area. "Over there, on the other side of the river," Kevin said, and watched his mom sweep the area with her torch. Fish darted away from the light.

"Are there any buildings around here?" she asked.

"No, not that I know of," Kevin said.

Daniel agreed with Kevin. "There was an old shed over the other side that gave access for the submarine cables. But it's derelict and it wouldn't be standing after the fire last week."

Kevin looked at his mother. She was thinking and searching the other side as far as the light from the torch would travel. She hoped to find something, something she had lost, something that was very important, but Kevin couldn't see anything. What could she have lost down here? Her face turned down in disappointment that she hadn't found what she was looking for.

Kevin saw her pain and said, "We can come back tomorrow and have a better look. I can show you how to get over the other side without having to swim across." She looked at him and for the first time since his grandparents died he felt a connection with her.

"Sounds like a good idea," Daniel said.

"Hang on. We can wade across now the crocs are sleeping," Tim said.

"What planet are you from?" Daniel asked. "There are no crocs here. He is just trying to scare you," he said to Jade. Daniel gave Tim a gentle brush up the back of his head.

"I suppose you're right," Callie said.

THE TRAIN PULLED into the deserted station. While it was still moving Shaun jumped off and started running home. Passing Kevin's house, he slowed to a jog; the garage door was open and he could see Kevin's bike propped up against the far wall, next to a jerrycan. He stood, thinking of knocking on the door to ask permission to borrow the bike. *Maybe they will let me.* He turned away, walked to the end of the street and turned the corner. For the second time in his life Shaun was immobilized with fear: his house, his home, was burning. He snapped himself out of it and as he started running, the front windows exploded. He ignored the heat, dug into his pocket and grabbed his key. The door was swollen and, no matter how much he tried, it wouldn't open.

Shaun rushed around the back of the house trying to find a way in, calling out to his dad. Shaun searched the backyard hoping his dad had stumbled out the back door. He screamed, *"Dad! Dad!"* ... no one came. Not a neighbor stirred. He was alone and screaming at the top of his lungs for help. He tripped, got back up and ran towards the drainpipe and started climbing. It was hot and he could smell his skin burning. He kept climbing.

KEVIN HEADED BACK to his dad's Dodge following the glow of torchlight as they swept across the dirt path. Hoisting himself up into the car he heard a cry for help. It sounded as if it was a street away on the other side of the vacant lot. It would take ten minutes to drive around. Daniel started running; Kevin jumped down and chased after him, with Tim following close on his heels.

"House fire," Daniel yelled to the boys.

Daniel, Kevin and Tim entered the street and could see flames over the top of the houses. Kevin knew the fire wasn't too far away, just around the next corner. They entered the next street and saw Shaun's house engulfed with flames.

Kevin saw Shaun in pain, rushing up the pipe, trying to avoid the flames.

"Get down," Daniel yelled. "Kevin, get the hose and aim it at Shaun and the pipe."

Shaun kept climbing; Daniel ran up to the house and wrapped his shirt around his hands and started to climb after him.

SHAUN SUDDENLY FELT someone hit his leg from behind, gripping his calf muscle and pulling him down. He hoped it was his dad. He looked down and saw Kevin's dad. Shaun's hands slipped and he found himself falling. It wasn't a long fall, but it seemed to Shaun to go on forever; he started to think of how many times he had fallen off the roof over the years. His back hit the ground and he couldn't catch his breath. He let himself drift, hoping he was dead, then he could see his mom and Rachel and tell them how sorry he was that he couldn't save either of them.

He passed out.

THEY COULDN'T HEAR any emergency vehicles. *Nobody was coming*, Kevin thought. He held the hose pointed at the house, feeling uneasy, his skin crawling. The air was getting thicker and he could feel mosquitoes biting at his neck. Even in the face of so much smoke they were determined to attack. "What are we going to do, Dad?" Kevin said, slapping at the bugs on his neck. "Shaun's dad must be in there."

"Something is terribly wrong, K. Look at that glow on the horizon. It's the city burning."

"Dad, we have to leave."

"I'm with you, K."

His mom pulled up, yanking on the handbrake, the Dodge screeching to a stop. She leapt from the truck with the first-aid bag, Jade close on her heels. They both went to Shaun. Jade watched him and Tim hose down the house using the neighbor's hose.

She looked around the street and he could see her noticing the empty houses, where no lights flickered and no curtains were drawn back.

"Where is everyone?" she said.

Shaun started to come around, trying to sit up, mumbling as Callie nursed his burnt hands.

"Shh, just relax. You're safe now," she said.

Shaun collapsed back onto the ground while Callie finished wrapping cold wet bandages around his burnt hands.

"You right to walk?" Callie asked.

"Sure. What about my dad?"

Nobody said anything.

"He's probably at the pub," Shaun said to them.

Callie and Jade helped him into the back of the Dodge.

"You're probably concussed," Jade said, putting on his seat belt for him. The boys jumped into the open back tray.

Daniel drove home. No one spoke as they pulled into the garage. Kevin stayed seated in the back watching the lowering of the electronic garage door locking out the world.

7

ECHOES OF THE DEAD: CASEY.
ENGLAND

"I'm going to make that rat's hole a hell of a lot bigger." Terry stood, dusting off the dirt, then picked up the mallet. Casey still lay on his belly, waving the torch through the opening. "You might want to move?" Terry suggested.

"What?" Casey turned and looked at Terry with the mallet, and sprang to his feet.

Terry swung, smashing the stone wall of the basement. It buckled. He swung again, a few stones dislodging and dropping to the ground. He cleared an opening wide enough for them to explore what was beyond the basement.

Casey ran upstairs for a second torch while Terry peered into the space beyond the wall. Running back down the stairs he nearly tripped on the last step, but managed to save himself from falling. They stepped through the hole into a chamber with two tunnels. Water was dripping down the wall rhythmically, pooling near their feet. Flickering, like fireflies, darted at the edge of the torch beams. They both shivered. In the corners, beyond the light, Casey caught a glimpse of a sudden movement. Terry turned to Casey knowing they had both sensed something, but neither knew what to say or do and chose to follow the beams of light.

Terry started off towards the tunnels, with Casey reluctantly following. Walking backwards to point the torch at the entrance Terry had made, he swept the light across the wall: *rats, just rats*. He turned, bumping into Terry.

"Where do you think this goes?" Terry said, stopping at the mouth to one of the two tunnels.

"Have no idea." Up on the wall near Terry's head, Casey saw an old hook with a bucket and a wooden baton fixed on the wall next to it. "What's that?"

"It's probably for tar. You'd dip the baton, then hit two pieces of flint together and ... let there be light."

"You missed your calling, you know that, don't you," Casey said. "Can we try it?"

"I don't think it would work," Terry said.

The light penetrated further into the tunnel, startling the rats out of the darkness. They rushed over and around Casey's feet. Terry jumped back, knocking into Casey and they both nearly fell on top of the rats.

Casey said with a slight smirk, "Just rats, Terry, just rats."

Terry held onto Casey's arms, acting as if he was helping him. "You right, pal?"

Casey decided to go along with him. "Yeah. A bit freaked, you?"

"I wasn't expecting them, that's all," Terry said, hiking up his pants.

The walls were cold and wet and getting narrower. The sound of bones crunching under their feet was like seashells. "Terry, we should go back."

"Just a little further. I felt a breeze, this has to lead to somewhere," Terry said.

Casey touched the cave wall, his fingertips slipping into

tiny indents that made the wall look like a giant sea sponge. Something splashed on him from above and he flipped his torch quickly upward. Within a split second his imagination took over and he saw saliva dripping from the fangs of a rabid bat, but the light revealed nothing more than an empty cavity. He could see Terry was getting ahead of him. He moved quickly to catch up. The tunnel widened into another chamber with more passages branching off.

Terry had stopped and was nervously scanning the walls. Shining the light as far down the tunnels as possible, while trying to hide his own apprehension, he said, "This is just going to keep going."

A stale smell, a metallic taste, sat heavy in Casey's mouth and irritated his nose. The sound of the dripping from the passageway became louder in his mind. There were pieces of wood and a jug protruding up from the ground.

"Alright," Terry said, looking over his shoulder. "I think you're right. I think for now this is far enough. We'll probably get lost if we go any further."

"This is a little freaky," Casey said. "Do you think we're still on the property?"

"Na, don't believe so." Terry turned around, thinking, looking left and right, then back at the jug. "Look at this old thing. Maybe it's still full of rum. What do you think, matey?"

Terry picked up a piece of the wood and started digging around the jug. He picked it up and shook it — empty. Under the jug, a bone was half buried, and he pulled and wiggled it until it came free.

"That doesn't look like a rat's bone to me," Casey said.

"Maybe it's not, maybe it's human," Terry said jokingly. He handed the bone to Casey. Casey looked at it; he didn't want Terry to think he was scared, because he wasn't treating him like a kid any more most of the time. But Casey hesitated, pushing his long curls up off his brow and out of his eyes. He rubbed his hands on his shirt. He knew he shouldn't doubt his feelings, but he wanted to go along with Terry, who was trying to be playful, a big kid.

Arm extended, ready to grab the bone, Casey dropped his arm to his side. "You know, on second thoughts, I'll pass. We should go back and check on Amy," he said, scratching his ear.

"Go on, it won't bite," Terry said, shoving it forward. "Take it."

"It could be diseased, or something," Casey said.

"What are you afraid of?" Terry playfully thrust it forward like a sword. Casey quickly sucked in his stomach, hoping it wouldn't touch him. Terry continued his banter, pushing it into the boy's chest. Casey seized the bone with both hands, trying to push it away, his body was instantly paralyzed and pain raced up his arm, into his shoulder. The sound of a young woman screaming filled his head, along with the image of her arm being ripped out of its socket. Casey's stomach exploded with pain, as she was kicked. The pressure on his lower back was horrific. He tried to move, heat crawled up his spine and he felt like his insides were going to drop to the floor.

Casey could barely hear or see Terry yelling at him to let go. He couldn't feel him wrestling with the bone, prying at his fingers, one by one until he let go. At that moment, Casey's body folded, dropped to the ground, and he grabbed his stomach and curled into a ball, crying.

Terry threw the bone away and it cracked as it hit the wall. "What the hell?"

He crouched down beside Casey and held him in his arms. Casey could hear him whispering like he had the first day he had found him lying on the road, reassuring him he was safe. He could see Terry's alarm and confusion. Casey was scared and skittish as if someone was there waiting, waiting to deliver another blow to his abdomen. He held tight onto Terry, hiding in his aura, not wanting to let go.

The feeling of being inside the woman's body was dissipating. He had never been so aware of how his own body felt until he couldn't feel it. He was grateful it had stopped. He was petrified, nervous, violated, and afraid it would start again. He slowly sat up with the distinct taste of blood in his mouth.

He watched Terry's hand lift to his own face, rubbing his eyebrows, concerned. He was trying to comprehend what had happened.

Terry brought his hand back down and patted Casey gently on his back, and asked him if he was all right. "What happened pal?"

Casey's torch was lying on the ground, shining down the right-hand tunnel; he thought he saw something move. He turned away and looked at Terry. He didn't know what to tell him. *He probably thinks I'm crazy anyway. That's not fair, Terry's not like that, he has always been there for me. What the heck.* "It belonged to a young servant girl, the bone. Her arm was dislocated, ripped out of its socket. She was malnourished, her bones were frail. She was beaten and kicked to death because she was pregnant with her master's child." Casey watched Terry's jaw drop. He didn't blink but he shivered, and Casey could see his Adam's apple bobbing as he swallowed.

Terry looked back towards the bone, then back at Casey, and studied his face. "How, how do you know this?"

"I don't know. It has never happened like that before."

"What *has* happened before?"

"You know, how like, when we were getting supplies at the baby store and I told you not to open the storage door. You did and the wolves were — well, you know. And then like, the book I gave you."

"I thought you were just having a lend with the book, and I thought you must have heard something in the storage room that made you cautious. I don't know much about this sort of stuff. Sorry, pal, Amy will know what to say. Hang on, does that mean we are really having twins? Never mind, I don't want to know."

Casey could see Terry was confused, but he didn't see any look of sneering judgement that an adult has when they think a kid is lying. He could see the worry in his eyes, his teeth clenched, thinking hard. Terry hauled him to his feet and dusted him off and Casey felt the man's strength and his need to protect Casey. He had never known his father, but he imagined him to be just like Terry. If Terry could've carried him, without embarrassing Casey, he would have. Instead, he looked down at Casey's feet making sure they were both planted firmly on the ground.

"Let's get you out of here to die another day."

Casey had to smile. "You think you're funny, don't you?"

"Uh huh. You right to walk?"

"Yeah." He held Terry's gaze, then at the corner of his eye he saw movement coming from the left passage and his eyes opened wide.

"What?" Terry said.

Casey leant closer and whispered. Terry bent down to hear. "We're not alone."

"The servant girl?" Terry whispered.

"No, don't turn, let's just go."

Terry picked up Casey's torch and handed it to him. Scared, they both acted as casually as possible, walking back the way they had come, trying to be rational and not run. Ducking through the entrance, back into the basement, they quickly dragged the old trunks across the floor and stacked them against the opening. They moved at a fast pace and raced up the stairs to the kitchen, locking the door behind them.

AMY WAS SITTING in the sunroom on a daybed. Even though the windows were boarded up, her head was tilted towards them, as if the sun was shining and warming her face. Sensing she was no longer alone, she opened her eyes. It took her a moment to focus and they stood silently. She looked to Casey like someone had just walked over her grave. Casey started to feel sick, bile rising into his throat. He felt himself go pale and gagged.

Amy jumped up. "Sit down," she said. She pulled him towards her and sat him down on the edge of the daybed.

His foot struck her book. He nearly tripped, accidentally kicking it open. "Sorry," he said as he continued to gag.

"Lean forward, put your elbows on your knees and your head in your hands, take slow breaths."

Casey did as she suggested. As he cast his eyes down they locked with the different letters of the open book. His mouth tasted of blood and he coughed violently, needing to spit. Amy passed him a tissue and he wiped his mouth, expecting it to be red with blood, so he was surprised when it wasn't.

"What happened to you guys, Terry?" She breathed out slowly as if she had been holding her breath. "Guys, someone has to let me in," she said.

Terry fetched two glasses of water, gave one to Casey and

sat beside him. Amy was pacing the room. "What happened, what's wrong? Are both of you going to just sit there and say nothing? I know something's not right."

Terry sat back against the sofa to lift his head towards the ceiling and then dropped it down, stretching it and rubbing his neck. "You'd better sit down," he said. He then proceeded to describe the events as best he could, although it sounded strange. Casey spoke up to explain what he had experienced and Amy's faced was mapped with confusion. She stood and paced up and down the room trying to comprehend what Terry had said. "Casey! You had a vision of a young woman's *death* by touching a bone that was centuries old?"

She looks worried. Casey could see her thinking, while he sat quietly on the lounge studying her face wondering what she was going to do. Surely they weren't going to keep him around once the twins were born; he was too creepy. They were probably regretting adopting him, and once the world got back to normal they would almost certainly send him to boarding school. Out of the corner of his eye, Casey saw a mist of energy move from the shadows and float into the hallway and up the stairs. The floorboard at the top of the landing sighed under some phantom weight, and they all looked in that direction, waiting, but there was only silence. Different smells wafted into the room, some pleasant, some not so. Amy looked like she was trying to focus on something that was hovering just out of sight. When the wind stirred outside, the windows behind the boards began to rattle.

"It's a tornado!" Terry yelled.

"They don't have tornadoes here!" Amy yelled back. The sound got louder as if a thousand pebbles were being pelted against the house.

Casey and Terry were on their feet and Amy was coming towards them. Casey witnessed the room fill with apparitions. Making a run for it, Amy scooped up her book from near Casey's feet and a circle of light radiated from the book, concealing them. Amy, Terry and Casey disappeared, becoming ghosts. Huddled together in the gentle whirlwind they saw people forming silhouettes, then colorful auras, and clothing from different time periods, moving around as if they belonged. A young woman sat in the side chair across the room and a man opposite her was smoking a pipe, the smell of tobacco filling the room. They talked and laughed casually.

"That couple are from the photo in the basement," Amy whispered.

Some of the ghosts look confused and lost, Casey thought. An old man kept repeating his movements, taking a book off the shelf and putting it back, taking it off the shelf and putting it back. A woman in a long black maid's dress with a white cotton apron walked into the room, seized the doorknob and walked backwards and closed the door. The door flung open by itself. The maid again walked into the room, seized the door handle, and walked backwards out of the room to close it.

"Those ones are just memories," he said pointing to the bookcase. "The people that keep repeating themselves are emotional memories. There is no stream of consciousness," he said.

"How do you know that?" Amy said.

He spoke in a low voice so as not to attract attention. "It took me a while to work it out, but after the river and my mom I thought I was a complete basket case. Take the flight over, for instance. You felt sick, right?" He looked at Terry, desperate for him to understand. "What you felt was the emotional memory of the person in that seat on the flight before you. It was his fear, his emotional energy he left behind. Like an imprint of a sweaty palm on a bench, or footprints in the sand. You're sensitive, Terry; receptive to other people's feelings. See that one by the kitchen doorway, not moving; the one with a beard and a frown, well that one is a lost soul, and he thinks he's still alive."

The windows stopped rattling, the projectiles against the house had ceased, and the apparitions flickered in and out, like a lost signal, a fading hologram. "The thing I don't understand is why I haven't seen my mom." Suddenly the room seemed vast as the apparitions vacated the space and went back into their reality. Casey stepped forward and the surrounding light disappeared. He looked back at Terry and Amy, scanning for a hint of what they might be thinking.

"They're gone but ..." Terry said, "... it feels like they're still here."

"I feel it too," Amy said.

"That's because they are, we just can't see them any more. They're in between the two worlds, ours and beyond."

"What two worlds?" Terry asked, following Casey into the kitchen.

Casey went to the back door and called for the dog. She didn't come. He called again, she still didn't come. The ground was littered with insects and they were embedded in the door.

Terry knocked them off the door and brushed them back outside. Casey and Terry circled the property, checking the house for damage while calling for the dog.

"She probably sensed the storm and took off for shelter," Terry said. "She'll come back. Don't worry about the dog. She will be all right."

They stepped into the kitchen and Amy pulled her

cardigan tight, as if a chill had passed over her body. "Close the door, Casey. We can't go anywhere, we have to stay here."

The thought of staying was terrifying to Casey, but the idea of leaving was worse. There was no hiding.

"Who's hungry?" Terry said.

Casey watched Terry rub his hands together and pull out pots and pans. Cooking was Terry's way of dealing with stress. The conversation about what had happened and what they saw was over. To be fair, they were handling it better than any adult he could think of. But he still didn't know what they thought about him being able to see beyond this world. He wanted to show them what else he could do. How he controlled the flow of energy, whether it was the lights, Amy's hairdryer, the stove or the car.

Amy stood next to the old wood-burning fireplace and watched Terry get the gas stove going. She moved towards him and held his arms softly, and turned off the gas. "I couldn't think of eating now. I can't believe what I just saw. We have to talk and Casey —"

She sat at the old wooden kitchen table and studied her fingers and nails. Terry hadn't moved. She turned to Casey. "What else do you see?" she asked him. "Do we survive this?"

Casey saw her eyes glaze over. "Amy, you're scaring me." He had never seen her look vacant, but Terry had and was scared too. Terry sat beside Amy to slowly rub her back. Casey leant against the sink and crossed his arms.

With tenderness, Terry said to Amy, "Look at me. Look at me, Amy."

She didn't take her eyes off Casey and said, in a robotic tone, "I know you can see things, Casey, and I want you to talk to me, I do. I want to help you make sense of what is happening to you. But the truth is, I don't really understand. It is so overwhelming, I don't know how to help you."

Casey had never seen Amy as anything but a tower of strength. He searched within himself for the right words to lift her from this dark place she inhabited. She moved slowly, like she was caught in mud, and it was encasing her. What could he say? He opened his mouth and let the first thing come out. "People have died and people are going to die. Maybe we all die tomorrow, I don't know. What I know is my friend Sophia is real and she is coming. Whatever happens, it will be the right thing."

Amy tumbled into the black hole. She said condescendingly, with a slight tilt of her head, "Your friend Sophia is a figment of your imagination. You conjured her up after your mother died so you wouldn't be alone. I get it. At best, after today your friend Sophia may be a ghost. I'll give you that."

Casey had wondered about it himself from time to time, thinking maybe Sophia was a ghost, or part of his own creation. "She is real, Amy. I thought that you of all people believed me."

"I believe you are emotionally sensitive and caring. Like when you took hold of that little kid's hoodie, seconds before he stepped in front of the car. His mother should have been holding his hand, and you knew that, and that's why you held him back. No other reason. Not that you saw the car before it came, or that he was about to step in front of the car, but that you were aware he was not being cared for by his mother, because you were missing your mom, and you are emotionally sensitive."

"I can't believe you, Amy. That's a load of crap, and you know it!" Casey's head started to hurt, his throat felt tight. His hands gripped his head, trying to stop the pain. "So that's what you thought," he yelled. "And you pity me."

Shocked, Casey felt his energy as a river that dragged him to its murky depths which then surged up and pumped through his veins. The kitchen lights started to flicker and the bulb overhead blew. Amy and Terry jumped out of the way as the shards of glass fell on the table.

Casey pulled the back door open and ran outside.

"Casey, stop," Terry yelled after him. "Casey, where are you going? Come back.

Amy, stay inside and shut the door behind me."

Terry saw Casey pass the barn and as he did the car and motorbike roared into life. Terry, confused, didn't know if he should stop and turn them off, or keep chasing Casey into the woods.

Tears blurring his vision, Casey tripped. He never realized Amy pitied him. All this time she was just humoring him. He couldn't believe it. He screamed and released his anger into the forest. The crows took flight and sticks and leaves started swirling around his feet, moving up and outward. The debris around him spiraled faster and faster. He didn't see how dangerous and out of control his behavior had become. A bad smell hung in the forest, the same smell that was in the house, but Casey was blind to his environment as he pushed his energy further and further away from him. He pounded his fist into the trunk of a tree and a shock wave vibrated into the ground, lifting the soil. It rocked fear into Casey.

Terry watched amazed at the growing force and chaos. He was worried Casey was going to get hurt unless he got himself under control. "Casey!" he called out. Terry hid behind his forearm, protecting his head and face and pushed through Casey's personal cyclone.

Casey faced Terry. A flying branch hit Terry on the side of the head, knocking him down. Casey heard the dog bark in the distance and everything went still, hovered in mid-air, and dropped. Casey felt electrified and exhausted. Then his senses focused on Terry and, horrified, he ran to Terry's side. He had never lost control in this way before, never hurt anyone. He had never wielded such power. He had felt detached and it terrified him. He bent over and brought up his lunch. Sophia was right — he had more power than he ever would have believed and he couldn't handle such power. He wiped his mouth and slid down by Terry's side and started crying. Terry wasn't moving. "I'm so sorry, Terry, please, Terry, I am so sorry. Please, please wake up." The dog and Amy came running.

"I am so sorry, Amy. Please wake him up." Amy was quick to act. She checked his breathing, running her hands along the top of his head. "He's got a bit of a gash just above his ear."

Casey sniffed back the tears, and nodded.

Amy resumed checking Terry's body from head to toe. "He'll be alright, Casey," she said. "He'll have a big lump on his head and a massive headache, but he will be okay. I'm sorry about before," she said. "You are my first child, and you're hardly a child. I have only had a year to get to know you and how to be a parent. I love you, Casey. This is very new to me and I handled it poorly. I am frightened, and I am sorry I hurt you. I saw what you just did and we will help you. You will learn to control it, or shut it down." Amy wrapped her arms around him and he dropped his head onto her shoulder and cried.

All the pain over the past year came flooding back. Terry started to stir and sit up. He gently placed his hand on Casey's arm. Casey felt the touch and lifted his head from Amy's shoulder to see Terry smiling at him.

"My head feels like it's being squeezed like a ripe tomato.

And since I'm the one that was knocked out here, what about saving some of that loving for me?" Terry said in a mock-dejected voice. Casey let go of Amy and threw himself at Terry.

The dog started to bark at the sky. They followed its gaze and saw the dense metallic cloud that appeared to be made up of tiny winged creatures swarming, moving like a snake with purpose, towards them. They hadn't noticed the sky turning charcoal, or that everything around them had darkened into shadows. An intense sickly smell was getting stronger.

"This isn't good," Casey said. "I think I attracted them."

Amy and Terry in unison asked, "How?"

Casey and Amy helped Terry to his feet. "Negative energy. I think it's the virus." They started running back towards the house, the dog leading the way. The beastly swarm came closer. The air thickened.

Inside, Terry dragged the table across the floor to jam it against the closed door. All the windows simultaneously started to rattle, and the wind whistled between the cracks. There was a crashing sound in the living room. Casey ran towards it and as he stepped into the living room, the boards against the windows moaned and distorted, bowed and splintered, yielding to the force of the wind. The windows erupted, the boards went flying. The stench magnified, and the swarm entered the room. It stopped, searching; it rippled like the movement of wind on the surface of a lake. It banked left towards Casey; it wasn't random they were heading straight for him. Amy grabbed his arm and dragged him back into the kitchen. Terry was right behind them, leaping down the basement stairs. The dog, thinking way ahead of them, barked at where the hole had been blocked.

"You're right, what choice do we have?" Terry said to the dog.

"Give me a hand, Casey." Terry's head pounded, trying to push the cases away to uncover the hole.

Casey placed his hands against the stack and closed his eyes, pushing with his mind. He heard Terry say "on the count of three".

"One, two —"

He put a little of his energy into his shoulder ready to push, but Terry never said three. Casey's eyes flew open, fearing the worst, and saw Terry standing clear of the suitcases. They had already moved and the hole was clearly visible.

Amy and Terry were quiet and still.

"Ah, good, good," Terry finally managed to say.

Terry picked up the torches and they moved into the tunnel. "Can you put them back across the hole from this side?" Terry asked.

"Maybe, yes." He again imagined in his mind the hole and the bricks that had filled it, and the cases piled high in front of it. Just the way it was when they first found it. He opened his eyes. He couldn't tell if the trunks were against the wall or not, because the cavity had been filled. They were entombed.

8

THE TALKING STICK: JADE. AUSTRALIA

The house was quiet when Jade crept out of Alex's room careful not to wake Kath and tiptoed into the hallway. She could see the light under Callie and Daniel's door as she moved towards Kevin's room. She stopped to listen.

"We have to go. We have to leave the city," Callie said. "If we can't find Shaun's family, we will have to take him with us. His hands will need to be cared for."

"Where do you want to go?"

"Saddleback Mountain. There is enough space, it has solar power, back-up generator, batteries — everything we need. My parents' belongings are there, including dad's light plane, a Piper Cherokee 6-300. Nothing has been touched."

Jade could hear Callie blowing her nose as if she had been crying. Feeling guilty about listening, she started to moved away.

"I have to tell you something about Ellen."

Jade was immediately glued to the spot.

"Ellen said, 'Hide. An ingredient has disappeared. I have failed.' Daniel, when she said it, I knew she was talking to me, telling me to run, to get out of the country and that's what I did, I ran. I watched them force her from the lab. She asked them where they were taking her and one of the two men, who had Russian-sounding accents, pulled her violently by the hair and pushed her towards the stairwell door. They were only inches away from the door to the bio unit where I was hiding and I held my breath. The man was telling her to stop asking questions, she would have plenty of time to finish her research. They opened the door and pushed her into the stairwell.

THAT'S WHEN I RAN. I wanted to go to her family, to the authorities. Instinctively, I knew I should run and not look back. I took what she had been working on and ran. I felt like I abandoned them. I also think whoever took Ellen killed my parents and have been looking for me ever since."

Jade started to cry silently.

"Why would you think that?"

"I never changed my passport from my maiden name. My mail still went to their place and my parents died a week after I returned. I think they, whoever *they* are, have been looking for me and I believe they have found us."

Jade backed away from the door and leant against the wall, trying to decide what to do next. She wiped her face with the bottom of her shirt before opening Kevin's bedroom door.

Jade pushed him gently, but Kevin was dead tired and didn't wake. She tried again and he woke with a start, nearly falling out of bed. Tim snored on, stretched out on the floor under the closed window. The full moon shone into the room, bathing them in the reflected light of the sun. The unity of the movements of the worlds fascinated her and she became absorbed in the essence of the moment, trying to forget what Callie had said.

"Jade, what are you doing?" Kevin said. She didn't answer. He waved his hand in front of her, casting a shadow across her face, as if he thought she might be sleepwalking.

"Stop doing that," she said. Jade watched him lean across to his side table and turn on the light. Kevin rubbed his eyes, waiting for them to adjust.

"How do you do it? I have to know," she said.

"Do what?" he said, sitting up and throwing his legs over the edge of the bed. He didn't have a shirt on and Jade admired his muscle definition.

"You work out?" she asked casually.

Kevin looked down at his chest. Looking self-conscious, he grabbed the shirt lying at the bottom of the bed and put it on.

"You have the body of an athlete. You should figure out what sports you like best. You will excel at whatever you choose. Anyway," she said, sitting and making herself comfortable on the floor in front of him, "you have to tell me how you do it."

"I don't know, Jade. It just happens."

"Nothing in this world just happens. We create our own reality; we are the cause of our lives. Let's say the thing just happens to you. Is it happening now? No. So there has to be certain criteria, a particular state or energy force that creates it. It's like the story about a mother seeing her child stuck under a car and she is miraculously able to lift the car. There is an energy force that comes from within her that enables her to do this. She is in a different state of being. What state of being is your body in when you are able to step through time?"

"I wouldn't say that I step through time. I don't know

where it is; it's not here, but it is. It's like running through the cavity between the inner and outer walls of a house," Kevin said, scratching his shoulder.

Jade twirled the ends of her hair and started running the soft end up and down her cheek like a paintbrush. "A corridor, perhaps. It didn't look like Earth, although it also did, just more vibrant. The colors were radiant and I saw Great Turtle."

"You saw what? A turtle?"

"My great-grandmother. So it can't be just out of your imagination. It has to have an existence in time and space. It seemed to be parallel to this reality. Tell me what your state was each time it happened." Jade studied him carefully.

Kevin looked deep into her eyes and he saw a flicker of light. "Do you wear contacts?" he asked. "I can see the light reflecting off the right side."

Reactively her hand shot up to her eyes. Wearing contacts was one of the changes she had made since her mother went missing, substituting the chunky black-rimmed glasses for them. "Yes, I do," she said feeling a little defensive.

"Are they uncomfortable?" he asked, mindful of Tim, asleep nearby.

"Not as uncomfortable as being teased for being intelligent. The glasses attracted negative attention. Now tell me, what was your physiological state when you created an opening and stepped out of our time and space?"

Kevin tilted his head slightly to the side nearly resting it on his shoulder. The ceiling was absent of answers. "There was always urgency. Trying to avoid something, to prevent a disaster occurring. I am still trying to work this out myself. What you heard me thinking about in, what shall we call it ... Kevin's world?"

"That's too egotistical even for you, K," Tim said sitting up. "Having a midnight powwow without me, are you. Who has the talking stick?"

"Go back to sleep. Don't mind him," Kevin said, looking at Jade.

"Actually, that may be very perceptive of him. Why did you say that: powwow and talking stick?"

"It's the first thing that came to me. I thought I could smell wood burning, which reminded me of a campfire," Tim explained.

"I am part Native American on my mother's side, my traditional name is Raven Wings. My great-grandmother, Great Turtle, was a medicine woman, a spiritual healer and could talk to the spirits in the afterlife. I had never seen proof of this until we disappeared in front of that wolf, into another dimension, where I saw Great Turtle watching us."

"Can we call you Raven Wings?" Tim asked.

Jade stuck her neck out and eyeballed Tim. "No!" she said firmly and turned to Kevin. "Tell me what state you were in when you opened the doorway."

"When I saw that boy drowning, nothing was happening to anyone. I was alone."

"Why were you there?"

"I wanted to swim and keep swimming."

He does that," said Tim. "He will jump in the pool at school and lap swim for over an hour and he will do the same at the river."

"Do you get into a rhythm?

"Yes, it's peaceful in the water."

"Do you swim when unhappy or upset, or when you're happy, excited?"

"Both, I've seen it happen." Tim's eyes widened, understanding. He knew why Kevin swam so much. "He is slow, swimming for ages, when he has a fight with his mom."

"Shut up, Tim." Kevin frowned at his friend.

"Let him speak," Jade said.

Tim stood up and paced in front of the window as if he was solving a riddle.

"Okay, Sherlock, lay it on us," Jade said.

"When he is excited, he swims like a rocket and splashes a hell of a lot, like a man possessed."

"So, K — Can I call you K?"

"Sure."

"What were you thinking about before you went to the river?"

"This is stupid." Kevin felt reluctant to admit he had been crying, and wanted his nanna to come back, and wanted his mother to hug him again.

"Come on. Look at this scientifically, an experiment."

"I wanted to see my nanna, I missed her."

"That's right! Soon after his mother returned from the USA, they were killed in a car accident on the way to his place."

"Tim, shut up!" Kevin growled.

"I know about your grandparents and I'm sorry," Jade said. "That was a bad time for us all. So you were upset, wanted to see your nanna and went for a swim. You dived into the river, but when you surfaced you saw a boy fall off a footbridge where usually there was no bridge. No footbridge ever existed where you swim, right. I think you dived into, and surfaced, in his time and space, becoming a witness. Did you go on the internet to search for the details?" Jade was getting excited and leant her body forward waiting for his answer.

"Yes, and there were no missing persons or death-by-drowning reports. There were weather anomalies across the world that day. Nature had a seizure. There was nothing I could find, the virus had washed up on our shores and the authorities thought my mind was infected."

Jade looked solemn, remembering her experience of that day, seven days after her mother went missing. "We are all connected." She reached up and pulled Kevin's pillow off his bed and lay on the floor with her legs resting on it. "Who's the pebble?"

"What pebble," Tim asked.

"The cause of all these effects. Everything starts in the Middle East."

"I thought you were a geek with a sci-fi brain," Tim said. "Thought you would believe in the Big Bang theory."

"I do, but who created the big bang, the one sonic clap, the one pebble. We are all connected: six degrees of separation." Jade had gone off into a spiral of thinking, believing there was something in front of her she wasn't seeing.

"When was the next time you stepped out of this reality?"

"Last week there was a fire."

"There was more than a fire, K," Tim said. "It was a scorcher of a day and we went for a swim; all good. I heard something on the other side of the creek, so I went to check it out. There was a bunch of dropkicks smoking and I hid behind a tree but one of them saw me and the next thing I knew was a fist ramming into my face and a foot stomped on my leg, hard, breaking it in two places."

Jade looked at his leg. "Impossible," she said.

"I know, right. We were burnt to a cinder from the sun when we came round and the whole place was ablaze. Kevin here made a splint for my leg while I was unconscious then dragged me to the edge of this wall. I kept passing out."

"When Tim didn't come back," Kevin interrupted, "I went to find him and saw Shaun and his mates beating up on Tim. They saw me and I was knocked out with a king-hit. Before I hit the ground, I saw the petrol bombs lined up, so I know Shaun and his mates set the bush alight and left us there to fry. I regained consciousness and before I opened my eyes, I could smell burning sage. My nanna used to burn sage and lemongrass. Then I saw the wall and couldn't see if Tim was breathing, or was it the other way round? I don't remember. The wall was a massive ripple of energy and I could see through it. It went to somewhere not part of this existence, but there was nowhere else for us to go, we would have died. Once we penetrated the wall's membrane and we were on the other side, Tim's leg was healed and the sunburn vanished. The fire engulfed us and we didn't feel a thing."

Jade sat mesmerized by the story. "You were healed? That's why, as soon as I stepped into the parallel universe, the atmosphere was calming and I didn't feel dizzy and my head stopped hurting. So when was the next time?" she asked.

"We were at the same place looking for the wall and couldn't find it. A couple of morons came around trying to pass themselves off as fire investigators. We knew they weren't and I freaked. That's when I saw a ripple, like a mirage. It wasn't in the same place as before, and this time we rode our bike into the rippling wall. We skidded around to face the men and it was evident they couldn't see us. They gave chase, but they couldn't see the wall, they couldn't see us, or hear us. I know they couldn't hear because this one didn't shut up," he said, thumbing towards Tim. "The rest you know."

"I think those guys have been looking for your mom.

Your mom thinks they might be the ones who kidnapped my mom. She said tomorrow we are leaving for Saddleback Mountain. Okay, I want you to trust me," Jade said, jumping to her feet.

"Wait, what, how do you know this?" Kevin asked.

"I heard your mom and dad talking as I snuck past their room. Come on, don't lose focus."

None of them felt tired. Kevin focused on the floor and noticed shadows moving quickly across the floor as if a full moon had moved into mid-heaven.

Jade stood behind Kevin and said, "Tim stand beside me." Tim rolled himself over the bed nearly hitting Kevin in the head with his ankle. Jokingly, Tim massaged Kevin's shoulders as if getting him loosened up for a boxing match.

"Stop it." Kevin slapped at Tim's hands.

Jade ignored Tim and focused on Kevin. "Now, close your eyes, and I want you to think about that day when you could smell the sage, and the fire was raging around you. How did it feel seeing Tim lying still beside you? What thoughts were going through your head?"

"This is sick," Kevin said.

"Relax, K." Jade watched Kevin's jaw tighten and flex, his breathing increasing. "How loud was the roar of the fire? How powerless did you feel?"

"You're making me feel like crap," Kevin said.

Jade fired off the questions. Kevin was feeling more and more helpless, wondering how he was going to get her to stop, when a hum, a low pulse and the sound of the rustling wind like slow-tearing Velcro entered into the room.

"What the hell?" Tim said.

"Shh," said Jade.

The scent of sage and lemongrass drifted past them. A metallic ripple of energy was forming in front of Kevin. A wall between two worlds. "Okay, Kevin, this is just a memory. You are safe in your bedroom with Tim standing right behind you and I'm standing next to Tim. Now open your eyes."

Tim couldn't hold himself back and blurted out mockingly. "He *loves* me." And held his hands to his heart and dropped onto the bed.

Jade whacked him on the side of the arm and he dropped the child's play. The three of them stared at the spot, as big as a basketball, shimmering in mid-air, a window in time. It wasn't a major opening, not like the other times. The energy flickered, folded into itself and disappeared.

"Awesome, K," Tim said.

"Alright," Jade said. "Now we know how you can create it. Next we need to see if you can choose your destination."

"What do you mean?" Tim said.

"She means, can we go anywhere within the universe?"

"Well, I was really thinking a little smaller, like how about this planet first," Jade said, tying her hair into a bun and sticking a pencil off Kevin's desk into it. "Like maybe we could go to my place. Maybe we could go back in time before my mom was kidnapped and warn her. There are so many possibilities."

"I don't think we can mess with time. I don't believe we should play around with this, we don't know what effect it has," Kevin said.

Kevin's bedroom door squeaked open and Daniel popped his head into the room. "Guys, it's been a long day. It's after one o'clock so get some sleep. Jade, back to Alex's room. It's going to be a big day tomorrow and we need to get up early."

Jade, embarrassed, scrambled out of the room, ducking

under Daniel's arm. Tim jumped back onto his makeshift bed under the window. Daniel smiled at Kevin. "Lights out," and started to close the door. Jade was halfway down the hall when Daniel said to Kevin, "Can you guys smell that?"

Holding onto the door handle of Alex's room, Jade whispered. "Sage." She smiled and walked into the bedroom, gently letting the door click closed behind her.

KEVIN WAS surprised he had slept so well. He lay still listening to the sounds of the morning when he felt his dad's big hand stroking his cheek softly and he swatted at it as if it was a fly, but his dad pulled his hand away quickly and Kevin smacked himself in the face instead. Tim opened his eyes just in time to see the impact and started rolling about with laughter. He was lucky he was already on the floor. Kevin threw himself out of bed and landed on top of him, and started punching him playfully in the ribs.

Daniel smiled, watching them for a second. Life almost seemed normal again. Then the smile fell from his face and he said, "Okay, you two, I need you to help me pack the car." The boys stopped wrestling.

"Where are we going?" He looked at Tim and back to his dad.

"We are all going. Tim, your mom and sister will come too, as well as Shaun and Jade."

"Where are we going?"

Daniel didn't need to answer. Kevin answered his own question. "Nanna and pop's, right? How did you convince Mom?"

"It was her idea. Now come on, get dressed and meet me downstairs."

THE DOOR to the garage was open. Tim recognized his hiking pack amongst the bags already lined up to be crammed into the cars. "Fair dinkum, nobody tells me anything," he muttered to himself.

"Your mom and Kath, about an hour ago, packed up a few things, and locked up your house," Daniel said.

"But what about my things?" Tim asked.

"Your mom knows what you need," Daniel said.

"No, there are things I want that she can't know because I don't know, so I know there're things that she doesn't know I want. I have to go to the house." Tim walked quickly away from Daniel to the front door and ran for home.

"Tim, get back here. Kevin, go get him."

Kevin chased, but didn't catch Tim before he reached home. He ran around the backyard, dug the spare key up from under the rock, and unlocked the back door leading into the kitchen.

"What are you doing?" Kevin yelled.

"Wait there. Hang on," Tim said.

Kevin looked around at the quiet street. He got a creepy feeling they were being watched. Across the road, Shaun's mates and Kath's boyfriend were coming out of a house. Tim stepped from the kitchen to see Kath's boyfriend swing his bat; the metal smashed the window of the car in the driveway. Kevin pulled Tim out of sight as he reappeared, awkwardly stuffing an old photo into his Velcro wallet. Jumping the neighbors' fence, Tim's shoelace caught in a crack, pulling his shoe off. Together they unlatched the runners and sprinted back to Kevin's.

"What was all that about?" Kevin asked, walking into his house.

"Nothing."

"Yes, it was. What gives?"

"It's a photo of my dad holding me when I was born. All right? Now shut up about it."

"Chill. It's all good. Don't sweat it."

Kevin followed the smell of pancakes. Jade was cooking with Alex's help. Molly played with her breakfast, dipping her jam toast into a bowl of rice cereal. She seemed to really enjoy sucking the cereal off the toast. His mom was sitting at the table applying a fresh dressing to Shaun's burnt hands. Shaun became agitated as soon as Kevin walked into the room and his mother looked up at him. Neither of them spoke.

She raised her eyebrows and Kevin shrugged his shoulders. They hadn't communicated like this since — he couldn't remember the last time. She tilted her head towards Jade and he nodded in agreement.

"Jade?"

Jade turned away from the stove and looked at Callie.

"Can you make Kevin a stack with lemon and honey to share with Tim, please?" Callie looked back at Kevin. "I'll call you when they're ready." She then nodded in the direction of the garage. Kevin knew what she meant. She wanted him to help pack the car. He said nothing and left the room. He was excited his mom was back, but afraid she would turn again. He decided he would be cautious in her presence; she was still the dragon lady.

IT HADN'T TAKEN long to pack up the two cars and be on their way. Tim looked like he had been crying. Kevin focused on the carnage out his window. His dad was in the second car with Tim's mom Sally, Kath, Alex and Shaun. Kevin was with his mom in the Dodge with Tim, Jade and Molly. Their car was out front. His mom steered around abandoned vehicles, tail lights flashing on and off. She turned off the main road, towards the coast, driving through the national park along the winding roads hidden under richly-scented vegetation. As they emerged out into the open, they could see the ocean on their left and as they rose to the top of a hill, Kevin could see the black cloud that hung over the city of Wollongong up ahead. His mom and dad stopped for Alex to use the bathroom at the lookout that was a jumping-off spot for hang gliders. Kevin could see the road winding below.

Thirty minutes later they entered the city and his mom slowed the car to a crawl. Tim said in a flat voice, "Look at that guy."

Kevin leant across to see out Tim's window.

"He looks like a zombie, without the blood drooling from his mouth. Why are they so pale?" Tim asked.

"I don't know," Kevin said.

"They probably don't sleep much any more," Jade replied. "Maybe they are low in iron, barely eat and just — keep wandering the streets, trying to remember what it is that they're supposed to do."

"It's so quiet, nobody is talking," Callie said. "There is no connection between anybody."

"Check out his pants, that guy's too, they look ..." Tim hesitated, searching for the right word.

"Soiled," said Jade.

Callie turned down a side street, away from the coast and towards Saddleback Mountain, some forty miles further south. The street was dark and looked cold. A shiver ran over Kevin's body. "What the hell?" A winged giant of a beast hovered before them, eating. The banging of the car's brakes as Callie tried to stop had no comparison with the crunching of bones and the horrific image of the little clumps of hair caught between the beast's bloody teeth. It slowly flapped bat-like wings while a scorpion's tail flicked wildly behind it, lancing into people on the streets. The town was its buffet. Each claw had a person skewered and ready to eat. Over the building tops the grotesque heads of two more beasts could be seen. This one was the biggest and stood at least four storys high.

Callie threw the car into reverse and took the side street they had just passed. Kevin, Tim and Jade swung around to look behind. Molly started crying. He saw his dad enter the side street, closing in behind them. Kevin flung around to see out his side window, leaning his head back to look up and felt the demon looking straight at him. He quickly pulled away from the window. The blood drained from his face, a chill filled his chest and warmth suddenly filled his bladder. Uncomfortable, unable to prevent himself from rubbernecking, he watched the beast swallow a man's bloody torso. His body became heavy with pain and dread. Suddenly, the creature's head and body exploded into a thousand tiny versions of itself: it became an angry swarm, and headed in their direction. Molly screamed louder.

Callie yelled, "Guys, face the front." The car jerked to the right, then to the left and the swarm, like a malicious pyroclastic cloud, raced up behind them. They didn't have a chance.

Jade's world spun, vertigo invading her senses. She slowly turned around to look at Kevin in the back seat and slapped his leg for attention. She was short of breath, pretending to be calm. "How do you feel now, K?"

Screwed, is the first thing that came to his mind. Kevin

knew what she was hinting at: where, where to, where to go? Then the image of the long driveway leading up to his nanna's home came into focus. *Of course.* He hadn't consciously done this before but he had to believe it was possible. He felt the black wolf start to circle and doubt found a voice laughing in his mind. He pushed it away, blocked it out, and listened to Molly wailing; the sound fueled his desire to succeed, to create a safe place for them all. He looked over his shoulder, making sure his dad was following close behind. The cloud, the shapeshifting beast, the swarm — whatever it was — was close and moving up and over his dad's car. Kevin saw his dad violently swerve his car from side to side in an attempt to shake it off.

"Call your mom, Tim," Kevin said, "and tell her to put it on speaker." The sound of the phone ringing was a strange sense of normalcy.

"Dad."

"K, not now."

"Dad, shake that thing off, you have to get closer, bumper to bumper. Or you won't be able to follow. I'm not —" The reception was lost. Kevin had no choice but to focus on the road out front, where translucent waves, a mirage, started to appear.

"What now?" Callie shouted. She butted her nose up against the windscreen and saw a sinkhole was opening, growing, in front of them. She started to slow and search for another way. Molly's screaming filled her head. Callie glanced into the rear-vision mirror. "Kevin! Quieten her down."

"No! Go straight for it!" Jade said. She leant over the gearstick and grabbed Callie's leg, pushing it down onto the accelerator.

"What? Stop it! Don't be foolish, we'll all die."

Tim pulled faces at Molly in vain. She couldn't be distracted. He looked behind him to see where his mom and Daniel were. They were still trying to shake the swarm. "Come on, K, you can do it."

Kevin was breaking out in a sweat and his face became red, his eyes sparked. There was no time for the car to brake or swerve. This time his mom would have no choice but to floor it, and hope they could jump the sinkhole. The car went straight up and hovered over and into the mirage. Kevin felt Jade's vertigo and anxiety vanish. He heard Molly stop crying and Tim's panic dissolve. Everything went quiet. They should have been alarmed, but they only felt peace.

They all thought they were on their way to the pearly gates, soon to see a bright light. The nose of the car tilted downward. They braced for impact, the world came alive, and the car dived into the dirt and gravel. Its back wheels thumbed the ground and the car slid out of control, sliding down the blue metal drive, straight for the veranda.

Kevin glimpsed behind. The doorway was getting smaller.

SHAUN BRACED himself against the leather seat in front and screamed in pain. Kath unlocked her seat belt and fastened his. Shaun felt feverish as every muscle in his body screamed with panic. He couldn't take his eyes off the beast. Everyone was freaking, he couldn't concentrate, his senses were locked on the entity. He knew he had seen it before in his dreams. It collapsed into a thousand mirrored pieces and headed towards them. Daniel was doing his best to shake it off, but Shaun knew they, he, had no hope of escaping this time. He was no longer an innocent boy. *This is*

Dad's doing, he thought. The memory of that night ten years ago came flooding back along with all the bad feelings, as if he was a kid again.

He understood his dad had violated his trust, and the trust of so many people, for some non-existent magical cure for his mom. He had loved his mother more than anything. He had prayed for her day and night to be healed. But what his dad did, whatever it was that he unearthed that night, seemed to be causing the extinction of humanity. The explosion, the plane to Egypt, the drug-induced flight, and the memories returned — the Russian in the palace. Everything had seemed so strange at the time. The dreams, the girl, finally it made some sense. It was her all along: Rachel. If only he could go back and stop his dad.

Shaun quickly turned away and faced front. The Dodge disappeared into thin air, just like Kevin and Tim had vanished at the river. What the hell? The swarm was descending again. Daniel swerved left then right in quick jerks.

A thousand vile angels swarmed behind the tail of the car. The swarm united, forming into one gigantic beast, stopping and sniffing the air as if searching for its prey. Filled with fury it turned from side to side in a rage. Its serrated tail sliced through the buildings and the people behind them on the streets. It shrieked and took off in flight.

The devil was enriched; his army of death was free to hunt. It exploded into a swarm of a thousand micro-beasts again, heading for the car. Sharp claws dragged along the boot of the car. Kath covered her ears, trying to block out the high-pitched screeches. Shaun saw the demons suddenly vanish behind them. The feeling of flying overcame him, and he relaxed. Every muscle, every cell was infused with light and peace. His burning hands cooled, the pain gone.

He was in slow motion, gazing over his shoulder through the rear window, searching for the swarm, and saw a horizon of green and blue mountains stretching to the ocean. As suddenly as it had begun, the floating sensation ceased, and the car fell from the sky. Shaun's body became heavy, and he was aware once again of the metal cage around them. The car landed heavily. Shaun's neck whipped back and his head smashed into the side window as the car slid along the gravel slamming into the rear of the Dodge. Hidden under a few layers of dust, the cars became one piece of metal beside the grazing cow.

9

LABYRINTH OF DARKNESS: CASEY.
ENGLAND

Sophia, are you there? Casey thought. Lying on the cold dirt floor on his back with his head resting on Terry's leg, Casey stared into the darkness. The chamber was musty. The air was stale. Terry was propped up against the cold stone wall and Amy leant against his shoulder. He could feel Terry playing with his curls; he wouldn't admit it out loud in a million years but Casey actually found it soothing. He shouted louder inside his head, *Sophia, are you there?* and Amy jumped a little. Casey was worried about Sophia because this had been the biggest gap between communications. *Maybe I could dream about her.* After sealing them in, he had tried again and again to break the wall down so they could get back into the house.

Amy had suggested they should just rest a while so he could build up his strength. "It will come when you're ready. You used a lot of energy in the forest beforehand. It might be best that we stay here and not go rushing back upstairs, for a while anyway."

Casey felt pressure building on his bladder. He closed his eyes and tried to sleep, directing his thoughts to his mom, her smile, the sound of her laughter and the smell of her perfume; he inhaled deeply to imagine the scent. Sometimes he felt so lost without her. *She would have liked Sophia — and Terry and Amy.* His bladder was becoming so uncomfortable his eyes flew open and he desperately looked for a place to relieve himself. *How long had they been here? Two hours at least,* he thought, looking back at the wall. He saw a shadow out of the corner of his eye; something was moving towards him. He closed his eyes, ignoring his bladder. He felt the presence getting closer and the darkness behind his eyes became intense. Internally, he tried to move away from the presence, slipping further away from his body, hiding in Terry's aura. He sensed it looking closely into his face, trying to see if he was awake. He kept as still as possible and felt like he was floating out in space. His heart was racing, but his breathing was relaxed as if in sleep. A breath crossed his face, and he nearly yanked himself out of hiding. He heard a voice in his head. His palms were sweaty. He disengaged from the separation of his body, feeling the intensity of the darkness move away. He allowed himself to float closer to the surface and open his stubborn eyes a crack. An apparition of an old man with ginger hair and a scruffy beard down to his chest, wearing a brown robe with a sash had disappeared into the wall. Casey's fear evaporated. He focused on the wall again and it moved like a Chinese block puzzle; he shuffled the bricks, restacking them. Casey slowly sat up, watching them move left-right and up-down. He reached out his hand to hold them and they succumbed to his energy. *I'm back.* Without touching them or moving from Terry's side he laid the bricks on the ground. He could hear the trunks sliding along the wall.

Terry and Amy were up on their feet beside him, motivated to step into the opening and back into the basement.

"What do you think, Terry?" Amy said. "Do you think it's safe? I don't feel the heaviness any more. It feels like a blanket has been lifted."

"Let me go upstairs first," Casey said.

Terry raised his brows and said, "No!"

"I hate to say it, but I think he's right, Terry."

"I'm not letting Casey go up there on his own!"

"Yeah, you should let me. You need to be here for Amy, and I'll know better than both of you if the entities are gone, or are hiding in the walls."

"Entities, is that what you saw? What do they look like, Casey?"

"They were metallic grey liquid like mercury. They had the snout of a dog, the wings of a bat, the tail of a scorpion, and death dripped from their mouths. They didn't have a stable, solid form. They fight for existence and that's why they need us: to possess our body and soul, leaving us only a corner of our mind to reside in. They have no souls, they're from hell. And to answer the questions you want to ask, Amy, I don't know how I know this stuff. Sometimes I feel like I am an old man who has lived a thousand lifetimes. But other times — well, you get the picture. I survived drowning that day for a reason. You found me, Terry, for a reason. This is all connected."

The darkness of the basement hid his face as he climbed the stairs. The golden retriever followed. Casey placed both hands on the door like in a fire and felt the silence.

He slowly pushed the door open and peeked into the dark kitchen. The sun had gone. They had been down there longer than he thought. Night hung over the house and his bladder was about to burst. He couldn't go slow; he had to get to the bathroom before his teeth started to float!

CASEY STEPPED into the kitchen and crept into the center of the room. He peeked into the lounge room; the edge of the curtain was possessed by a pre-dawn breeze. A fog drifted through the open window and Casey shivered. The wooden panels that had hung over the window lay by the bookshelf and the side table, lamp, and chair were knocked over. Casey stood with the dog by his side in the middle of the room, testing for a sense of any other presence in the house. It seemed quiet and empty. He flicked off the light switch and waited. Nothing: no lost souls, no apparitions, no emotional memories. Something had taken them away. It had become eerily quiet and empty. He walked cautiously into the foyer and flicked the light up the stairs. Satisfied he was alone, he entered Amy's great-aunt's old room where she had stayed during her final years. He wanted to use the bathroom and closed the door slowly behind him, hoping to reduce the sound of the squeaking hinges. The torch clanged as he laid it on top of the porcelain. He quickly unzipped his pants and sighed in relief as the stream went on forever.

Casey zipped himself up, washed his hands and opened the squeaky door. The sound unnerved him, making him feel silly. The floor was loud, and the room smelt musty, but it felt happy and comfortable, and he imagined this was how Amy's great- aunt was. The thought of frying up eggs and sausages, a Sunday English breakfast, made his stomach rumble. The clock in the room chimed, signaling dawn and the sun's imminent rising. *Where has the night gone? Where is Sophia?*

Casey walked back to the basement passing the dog that patiently waited for him. She stepped in behind as he reached for the door handle. Suddenly the door was pushed inwards. He let go, stumbling backwards over the dog.

"What the ..."

Terry emerged from the darkened doorway. "Why are you on the floor?"

Casey, Terry and Amy laughed nervously.

"What the hell took you so long?" Terry asked.

"I had to go to the bathroom. It's all clear."

"What's clear?" Terry said. "The house or your bladder?"

"Funny! The house. It's just a bit of a mess."

The dog scratched at the back door, so Amy let her out. Five minutes later it scratched at the door, wanting back in. It settled on the kitchen floor and slept for the next few hours while Amy, Terry and Casey cleaned and secured the house. Terry and Casey boarded the windows and Amy tidied up. Light started to shine under the back door. There was no point in going to bed, they were all hungry anyway.

"Let's have breakfast." Terry fired up the stove and Amy pulled out the sausages and egg powder. Casey made the toast. They worked together as a team, not talking but enjoying the ordinariness of preparing breakfast.

IN A LABYRINTH of darkness Joe watched Sophia glow while she slept restlessly. Stunned, he looked on in silence.

Beads of sweat sparkled on Sophia's forehead like jewels. She was the only source of light in the dark tunnel. Slowly she started to lift off the ground, then gently as a feather floated back down and the glow dimmed. Father McDonald kept murmuring his prayers and Joe joined in and whispered his own. Together, they begged God to give her the strength to do His will.

Father McDonald switched on the torch. Joe covered his eyes to shield them from the artificial light, watching Father McDonald pop a tiny pill into his mouth. Rubbing his chest he said, "It just needs to keep ticking until this is over." Then he leant over to Sophia and whispered, "Sophia, it's time to wake up. We have to get moving."

Joe packed up the rubbish of their snack bars as the torch flickered, unnerving him. It was the last torch. Sophia dusted herself off and silently they continued walking. The tunnels narrowed. Two hours passed before the torch flickered again, and the light was suddenly gone.

Father McDonald pushed the light on his watch and said, "Have trust, Joe, we will be out of here soon. I feel it in my aching bones."

Joe thought he could hear the sound of water drip, drip dripping into a pool. *Pinpointing sound in the tunnels is difficult.* He walked on, took three steps, then dropped into a body of cold water.

"What was —" Father MacDonald said.

It's too late to stop them. They were walking so close. Joe felt the weight of Father McDonald, followed by Sophia, falling on top of him, driving him under. The backpacks weighed them down. Joe started to panic. Father McDonald's head went under the water and he stretched his arms out to Joe, shining the tiny light from his watch. Joe saw the dot and struggled to the surface.

The light went out. Under the water, Father McDonald struggled out of his backpack. He splashed to the surface. "Let go of the bags."

"We won't survive if we let go of the packs," Joe said.

"Joe, let them go. We have no choice."

"Oh God." Joe slipped one arm at a time out of the harness. "Sophia, hold onto my shoulders and don't let go.

I'll get us out of here." He didn't want to turn, he didn't want the light, he was afraid of what he might see.

"I'm a good swimmer, I am right behind you," she said. "But Joe, what about your prosthesis?"

"It's an Aqualeg, an amazing invention. I can do everything I did before I lost my leg. Now stay close, hen. Both of you stay close. After this, I think a warm fire with good friends and a whiskey might be in order."

After ten minutes, the water felt as if it was now freezing over. Joe breaststroked slowly in front of them hoping he was not leading them in circles. *We have to get out of here.*

Father McDonald said, "I suppose we could think of this as an extended baptism."

"Or a mikveh," Joe said, shivering.

Sophia's teeth were chattering. If there had been light, Joe would have seen that her lips and under her eyes were purple. "What's a mikveh?" Sophia asked.

"It's an opportunity to cleanse your spirit of any negative energy that you may have collected. The mikveh is a body of water that is connected to the flowing waters of mercy that come out of Eden. The ocean is a perfect place for a mikveh. You meditate on the layers of your spirit, or aura, being cleansed while you bob up and down under the water eleven times or more."

"I love the idea of the ocean but I have never seen it in real life. One day, Joe, I would like to go to the beach and maybe we can do a mikveh together," Sophia said.

"Ah, shit!" Under the surface of the water Joe hit his leg on something hard.

"Okay, maybe not," Sophia said.

"Ah, no, hen. I hit my knee on a rock." He reached under and felt around, finding a rock ledge. He pulled himself up onto it and crawled on his hands and knees until he slapped dry land. Joe climbed out of the water, then walked back, careful not to slip, and lifted Sophia up. They both fumbled in the dark for Father McDonald's arms. Joe seized Father McDonald's cold skeletal hands and pulled his dead weight up and onto the rock. They all sat on the edge.

Father McDonald pushed the light button on his watch and the chamber's darkness was penetrated by the faintest glow. Using the light, he awkwardly tried to force his hand into his wet pocket.

"What are doing?" Joe said.

"My pills. They're gone."

The roof was invisible beyond the reach of the light. Joe helped him up and they started shuffling over the rock onto solid ground. The cave walls were opening out. Joe felt Sophia, at his back, hook two fingers into his pants belt loop.

"Stay close, hen." Joe walked with his arms outstretched, feeling for obstacles and hit another wall. His heart beat faster; he thought he had reached the end. They had been travelling for days. *This can't be it.* He felt along the walls. "Sophia, let go, and stay where you are." He shuffled his feet a few steps to the left and hit a wall. He then shuffled to the right and there was another wall, a dead end. He wanted to weep, but placed his forehead against the cold rock, his arms outstretched, touching each side. The tips of his fingers on his right hand slipped into a crevice. He moved them deeper into it, not daring to move any other part of his body. He could fit in his fist; he opened his palm, and turned his body towards the gap and measured the space with his hands.

"Father McDonald, turn your watch light back on, please."

Sophia and Father McDonald moved up beside Joe.

There was a gap, hardly big enough for Joe to fit through. Sophia would fit. Side-on, they all might be able to squeeze through. Where would it take them? Joe wondered. He smiled at his two companions. "What do we do?"

"We keep moving forward," Father McDonald said. He let his light fall dim and waited for Joe to lead.

One by one they slid into the suffocating space. The darkness was getting to Joe; frustrated, he wanted to scream out loud. He thought of Sophia and how brave she was. He reached back and searched for her hand and held it tight. He sucked in his belly and kept shuffling to the right.

"You know, Joe, every turn we have made is to the east," Sophia said.

He stopped shuffling, breathing heavily. "Really, I'm going to resist the urge to ask you how you know that."

Time was non-existent and the darkness was making Joe feel a little crazy. He stopped again and looked at his hand against the rock and thought he could see it. He held it up in front of his face and was able to detect a faint outline. He looked back at Sophia and could identify her shape. He shuffled forward, urged on by the possibility the light was just around the next bend. It was getting tighter and the rock scraped against his belly, ripping his clothes. He squeezed around a sharp narrow corner past a protruding boulder into an opening of blinding light. Instinctively, he covered his eyes. "You're going to have to let your wee eyes adjust, hen. It's bright."

Sophia and Father McDonald followed him into the open, shielding their eyes. A stream of light from above shone down into the middle of a domed cavern. Beyond the hole in the ceiling was the sky. Their movement disturbed the wildlife nestled amongst the cracks in the cavern's walls. Hundreds of birds took flight, chirping and squawking, spiraling up and escaping into a clear blue sky. It was a magnificent sight. With their heads tilted back they watched in awe as the birds flew into the streaming light. The cave went silent. Joe reckoned himself to be trapped in the pit of a lion's den. He looked at Father McDonald who was holding his chest trying to catch his breath. He dropped his hand to his side aware of Joe's gaze.

Father McDonald squeezed out a few words. "Smell that? That's the smell of fresh English air."

"How do you know we didn't make our way to the tip of Scotland?" Joe asked, sitting on a boulder. "Don't look at me like that, hen, I'm just resting me peg. I suggest you two do the same."

"Scotland has a sweet fragrance of life that warms your heart in the coldest of winters. That's how I know we must be in England," Father McDonald said.

"Come on, we have to push on. It's not much further," Sophia said. But the men weren't budging. Sophia sat down and wrapped her arms around her legs trying to warm up. "Okay, five minutes." Her clothes were drying slowly, but she knew a warm bed awaited, and a breakfast Joe would die for.

THE AIR through the opening in the cave ceiling was sending a chill down Sophia's spine. They had been resting for fifteen minutes, but it seemed to her like ages. She was feeling the cold more and more and just wanted to get going again — they were so close. Off to her far right a shadow moved and she turned her head as slowly as possible. The figure was familiar, an animal. It looked like the deer and it knew she had seen it. It turned down a tunnel on the other side of the cave. Sophia got up. "We have to go now. Joe, help

Father McDonald. Follow me," and she ran off after the deer.

"Wait, Sophia, don't run off like that," Joe said.

Sophie walked closer to the deer. Every step she took made noise and she was afraid she would scare it off. She reached out her hand and it was gone. Joe and Father McDonald came up behind her.

"What is it?" Father McDonald asked. The three of them stood waiting for their eyes to adjust to the new darkness. The smell of salty air had penetrated down the musty tunnel.

"It's not far now," she said, looking at Father McDonald. "Casey knows we are coming. The others are together. They are tired and scared but safe for now." They moved in silence. Joe had given up questioning her. *His life, all our lives, have changed so much.* She knew what it was like to lose the people you loved and felt his heartache. *If we could only live within our dreams we would be happy and live a thousand lifetimes in a single night. He lost his best friend and brother.* She reached out and held Joe's larger hand.

"Can you smell that?" Joe said. "That smells good." They walked into another tunnel, another chamber.

"Casey was here," she said, looking at the jug and bones on the ground.

"Who is Casey?" Joe finally asked.

"He's my friend. That's who we are going to see. He's from Utah."

"Utah in the US of A? But, hen, we haven't left the country. At best we are near the Holy Island."

"That's perfect, Joe. I knew you could do it. God sent you for a reason. To be the navigator."

"That smell, it smells like a breakfast bar."

"Is Casey still here?" Father McDonald asked.

"Not in the caves," she said, "but I can feel something else. He was upset, something about a dead girl."

"Oh, shiver me timbers, hen, we'd better get a move on, so we can help."

"No, we can't help. She died a long time ago." They walked on and Father McDonald stepped into another cavern, and into and through another tunnel. "Over there," he said pointing, "up ahead."

"What?" Joe said. "Something smells good."

Sophia could see the ginger-bearded man in medieval robes passing through a wall. "I see him."

"Who is 'he'?" Joe said. "I don't see anything."

"I don't know," Sophia said. "Can you see him too, Father?"

"Yes, yes, I can Sophia."

They moved towards the wall and Joe followed his nose and found the opening into the basement. The smell of fresh eggs and toast drifted down the stairs.

"What if we are in the wrong place and the people on the other side of that door aren't friendly, after all? It could be a base of infected soldiers."

"Have you seen any of the infected eat?"

"At the beginning, yeah. I couldn't tell them apart until they got violent," Joe said.

"Okay, Joe, you go first," Father McDonald said.

"No, it's not necessary," Sophia said.

"If it's not necessary, why are you whispering?" Joe asked.

"I, I don't know. You started whispering first," she said.

CASEY WATCHED TERRY COOK. He was currently working at

shaking the pan to keep the scrambled eggs from sticking. He had made porridge with stewed rhubarb as well as kippers with fried tomato and toast. He scraped them into a dish then searched for a place on the table. Terry looked at all the food and shuffled a couple of plates around to make room; he realized he'd overdone it.

He looked at Amy. She was looking at him with a smile. "Hope you don't think we three are going to eat all of this?"

Terry was wearing Amy's great-aunt's apron and wiped his hands on it. He scratched his head. "I don't know what I was thinking," he said. "How wasteful. We should be conserving the food. Look at me acting like nothing is happening."

Amy got up and hugged him. "It's okay," she said, picking up a plate and kissing his cheek before spooning scrambled eggs onto it.

Casey felt Terry was tearing up. It was all starting to get to him. "Don't worry, Terry. I promise you all this ..." Casey said, waving his hand over the table like a magician, "will be gone in no time and —" Casey stopped speaking. They froze and looked towards the basement door. The stairs creaked. The dog started to bark. Casey pushed back his chair and stood up.

"Hush," Casey said and tugged at the dog's collar. The dog growled at the door.

Terry stood in front of Amy and looked back at her and Casey. "What now?" Terry whispered. "God, please, give us a break." He turned back to the basement door. *Bang bang bang*. All of them jumped with fright. The dog barked. Nobody headed for the door. Terry turned to Amy and Casey indicating for them to go into the other room and hide, but neither of them budged. He picked up the frying pan. The handle started to turn. A big wet dirty man stood at the threshold. Terry waved the frying pan up in the air, like a batter waiting for the pitcher to throw the next ball. He watched the big fella eyeballing Amy and Casey.

"You Casey?" he said in a thick Scottish accent and nodded to the boy.

"Who wants to know?" Terry said.

"Yes, I'm Casey." He stepped around the table out of Terry's reach.

"Casey, get back. What are you doing?"

"I have someone who wants to meet you," the intruder said, stepping aside.

"Don't you come any closer. Who are you, and how did you get into the house?" Terry didn't take his eyes off the man. "Casey, do you know this man?" Terry was at his wits' end, tired and hungry, endorphins from the last twenty-four hours starting to ache in his muscles, and the frying pan was getting heavy.

"My name is Joe," he said. "I have a strange wee lass who believes you are expecting her."

Terry looked at Casey; they held each other's gaze.

"Where is she?" Casey asked.

"*Sophia*. Come up here."

They could hear a mixture of delicate and shuffled footsteps climbing the stairs. There was more than one person. He couldn't hold the pan up any longer. Amy put her hand on his arm and it collapsed by his side.

Joe said, nodding to the table, "Looks like the lass was right. Looks like you were expecting us. I could smell it for the past five minutes."

Amy stepped around Terry. "Please, sit. Where are my manners?"

Terry kept one eye on the big fella and the door. Coming out of the darkness, Sophia stepped into the kitchen. She was wet, dirty and skinny, in need of a good meal. Despite that, her long wavy golden hair shone like Amy's when caught in a summer's rain. She had rosy lips and cheeks and she was beautiful. Casey had tears welling in his eyes as he looked at Sophia. Together they smiled, and gave a little chuckle. Casey was entranced and slowly walked over to her and she hugged him. Terry couldn't resist; he approached Sophia and squeezed her arm to check she was real.

"I'm real," she said.

He pulled his hand back and looked over to Amy, who was staring at Sophia as well. Suddenly there was a cough from behind her.

"Sorry, Father," Sophia said, moving further into the kitchen and stepping aside. There was a tall, frail man behind her. Terry grabbed a chair and sat him at the table before he collapsed. "Are you okay? You don't look well."

"Please, everyone come in, help yourself. My name is Amy, this is Terry and, well, it seems you know Casey."

Joe and Sophia went to the sink and washed their faces and hands. "Why are you rinsing them three times?" Casey asked Joe.

"My grandfather used to do that," Amy said. "Casey, get the man a clean hand towel from the drawer next to your right leg."

"How did you find us?" Terry said.

"Joe," Father McDonald said.

Joe blushed. Regardless of his size, Casey thought, he seemed harmless.

"Do you mind if we could dry off our clothes?" Joe asked.

Casey ran upstairs and fetched towels for them.

"Thanks son," Father McDonald said, drying his clothes before draping the towel around his shoulders.

Casey couldn't quite believe what was going on. As they

sat down to eat, Joe helped himself and began telling them how he had met up with Sophia and Father McDonald. How they escaped the giant hooved creatures; that the evil eye was searching for them. Amy told them about being visited by demons and wandering spirits that were starting to appear more often. She also mentioned what happened in the barn and how he had glowed and used telekinesis to rebuild a wall to protect them. Everyone was talking at a hundred miles a minute, spilling details of every danger they had come face to face with over the past few months.

"These eggs taste so good," Joe said.

Sophia was enjoying the porridge with rhubarb and Father MacDonald had his hands wrapped around a warm cup of tea. The worst, Casey thought, was the shooting at the church. Sophia told the story with such sadness, his heart ached; and she believed it had been her fault. Casey could see Terry on the edge of his seat, wanting to pick her up and protect her from all the evil that she had seen. Sophia was mesmerizing. He supposed he had fallen under her spell over a year ago when he first saw her in his dreams. He was surprised how much she looked like Amy.

Terry started clearing the dirty dishes off the table and Joe stood to help. "No offense," Terry said, "but you guys could focus on a bath."

"Right you are," Joe said, taking a whiff of his armpit.

"The challenge is going to be coming up with some clothes for you," Amy said, leading them out of the kitchen.

Casey started clearing the table. "You go help Amy," Terry said. "Go practice whatever you call it, do your thing. And make a few quick beds."

Casey smiled and headed out of the room, but not before Terry whipped his behind with the wet end of the tea towel.

"Oi, that hurt," Casey said, rubbing his butt.

"*Oi, that hurt,*" Terry mimicked, enjoying their play.

"You must be tired, and dreaming of a warm shower," Amy said.

"You smell like you've been buried alive," Casey said.

"What sort of comment is that?" Amy said. "And how do you know what it smells like to be buried alive — no, don't answer that."

"I just meant they smell of dirt and murky water laced with sweat."

Amy crinkled her nose and shook her head. "Only a boy would say something like that. Come on, everyone, let's go upstairs and rustle you up some clothes. Then you can shower."

Terry placed a supportive hand on Father McDonald's elbow. "Are you okay with the stairs?"

"I'll be fine. Just need to go slow. I will be much better after a good sleep."

"I'll help you, Father," Sophia said, taking his arm.

10

ORDER AMONGST CHAOS: JADE.
AUSTRALIA

Daniel took off his seat belt and asked, "Sally, are you okay?" as he reached back between the two front seats to check on Alex as well. He could feel Sally's arm moving against his, and he could see Kath and Shaun in his peripheral vision. Alex was conscious, and didn't appear to have a mark on him. His little face looked like it was about to crumble into tears. "Did we crash-land in heaven, Daddy? Did nanna and pops ask God for their house to go to heaven, too?"

"No, mate, you can't take things like houses to heaven," Daniel said.

Daniel looked at Kath. "You okay?"

"Freaked. Where did that house come from? Where are we? What happened?" Kath said.

Daniel checked Shaun. His head was flopped over and bleeding. "We are at the foot of Saddleback Mountain at Alex's nanna and pop's house. Isn't that right, Alex?" He wanted to hear him talking to know he was still okay.

"Yes, Daddy."

Shaun was unconscious and had a massive lump on the side of his head.

Kath looked out the window as if they were on Mars.

"Sally, talk to me," Daniel said. "Kath, sweetie, listen to me, can you move okay? Can you check on your mom?"

Kath slowly got out of the car, steadied herself and pulled her mother's door open. "Mom, Mom, you okay? Show me — show me your face. Ah — that's got to hurt."

"My face really hurts. I think the airbag broke my nose."

Daniel pulled himself back between the two seats and took a look at Sally. Her nose was broken. "This is going to hurt, but it will be quick."

Sally screamed as Daniel cupped his hands around her nose and snapped it back into place.

Daniel got out of the car, rechecked Shaun, then gently moved him from the car and laid him on the ground making sure his airways were open. "Watch him," he said to Kath.

Daniel lifted Alex out of the child seat and sat him on the grass next to Shaun. "If he wakes up, Alex, tell him he has to stay still. Can you do that?"

Alex nodded.

Daniel approached the Dodge where he saw Callie slumped over the steering wheel. His stomach tied in knots. "Callie, Kevin, you okay in there? Answer me, Cal." Kevin opened his door and stumbled out, carrying Molly. Tim was close behind. "You all right, mate?" Daniel asked, placing his hands on Kevin's shoulders. He held him at arm's length and looked into his eyes then checked Molly. Satisfied they were fine he scanned Tim's eyes and body; he too was all right. *This is incredible,* Daniel thought. "Go help your mother, Tim. She's okay, just got a bloody broken nose."

"No need to swear, Mr D."

Daniel walked around to Callie's door, staring back at

Tim. "You're not squeamish with blood, are you, mate?" he said, opening Callie's door.

"No, I'm good as long as it's not mine," Tim said, getting out of the car.

Callie's and Jade's airbags had been released. Jade's head had been pushed back into her seat and he was afraid that the blow of the exploding bag had snapped her neck. He checked Callie's pulse. She was alive. He reached over and felt for Jade's and she started to stir.

"Don't move, Jade. Don't nod or shake your head, keep still until I come over and check you. Can you do that for me?"

"Yes," she whispered. Her eyelashes glistened. "You need to make sure I haven't snapped my neck, don't you? I can feel my fingers and toes."

"That's great, Jade. Just keep still for me. I'm checking on Cal ... she's unconscious. I'm just going to check she is breathing okay."

He carefully moved Callie's head back against the head-rest. No bleeding from the ears. Her left eye and cheek was swollen and the airbag had knocked her out cold. He pushed her hair off her face and lifted her eyelids, checking her pupils. She started to come around.

"How you doing, Jade? Not much longer."

JADE KEPT AS STILL as she could. Everything in front of her was like looking through a kaleidoscope. She wanted to move and wipe away the tears. Even though she was scared she was impressed. She was facing a pretty, blue-grey two-and-a-half-story house. White window frames and a large homely wrap-around veranda. A cane chair hanging on the veranda was swinging slightly. They were in the country! *Kevin has an incredible talent.*

"How are you, Cal?"

"Sore, like I fell on my face."

"Wiggle your fingers and toes for me. Does it hurt anywhere? Look at my finger, any dizziness?"

"I think I'm dreaming. Is this a dream?" "Why do you think you're dreaming, Cal?"

"Because we're butted up against my parent's veranda forty minutes away from Wollongong?" Suddenly she sat up and whipped her head left and right searching for the swarm that had chased them. Her eyes widened, memories flooding in. "The beast, the swarm, where is it? The kids, Daniel, the kids!"

"Keep still. No sudden movements, we're all safe. How did you do it, Callie? How did you get us here?"

"I don't know. I don't know what happened."

"It was Kevin," Jade said, still rigid in her seat, only swiveling her eyes in their direction.

"What? Kevin, how?" Daniel moved around the front of the car yelling back at the others. "Sally, Kath, Alex — how are you guys doing?"

"Shaun woke up, Daddy. Kath said if he moves she's going to sit on him."

"I don't think that's a good idea, Alex. Maybe you should keep an eye on both of them."

Jade tried hard not to laugh, afraid of moving. It was all so absurd.

"Okay, Daddy."

Out of the corner of her eye, Jade saw Sally come up on Callie's side of the car holding her nose. "I'm all right, Daniel. How are you, Cal?"

"Could be better."

Daniel opened Jade's door and went through the same procedure he'd probably done a thousand times for car crash victims.

"You seem uninjured," Daniel said. "Although without an X-ray I can't be a hundred per cent sure."

Callie was already getting out of the car, ignoring his protests. "Jade, sweetie, are you okay?"

"I'll be fine," Jade said, slowly moving and rubbing her neck.

Kevin, with Molly in his arms, came up on Jade's side of the car. Callie walked around and hugged Kevin and Molly as one, before taking the baby into her arms. Kevin stood there as if stunned, but automatically reached out his hand to Jade and helped her from the vehicle.

Alex shouted, "I'd give you a hug, Mommy, but I have to watch Shaun."

Callie went to him and affectionately ruffled his hair. Jade saw the way Kath was looking at Shaun. Callie passed Molly over to Kath and said, "Take care of her, will you," as she knelt by Shaun and went through the same procedures as Daniel, making sure there was no bleeding or symptoms of internal damage. He was obviously concussed and had a gash on his head.

"Do you think you can sit up?"

"Yeah ... my hands — they don't hurt." He sat up and started to pull at his bandages with his teeth. "Take them off," he said, in between biting at the bandages. "Take them off."

"Shaun, you need to leave them on. It's going to take a few weeks for them to heal," Daniel shouted.

"TAKE THEM OFF."

Callie frowned and moved away.

"Hey, mate!" Daniel said. "That's no way to talk. If you

want them off that badly, okay. But you won't be able to do anything and it's going to hurt like hell if you knock them."

"They don't hurt any more," Shaun said. "They just stopped. One second they were on fire and then they just stopped hurting."

Daniel unwrapped Shaun's right hand and Callie unwrapped his left. They both slowed as they removed the final strands, careful not to rip the wet gauze too fast.

"This is going to hurt a bit," Callie said.

"No, no, it won't. It doesn't hurt any more." Shaun jerked his hands away and the final bandage fell to the ground. His hands were healed. There was no sign of the burns.

"Just like my leg," Tim said. Tim flinched as Kevin nudged him in the ribs.

Callie and Daniel were flipping and rubbing Shaun's hands, over and over. Shaun smiled. Jade thought it was the first time she had seen him smile.

Tim said quietly to Kevin, "Why have his hands healed, but his head is still bleeding, and my mom has a broken —?" Kevin elbowed him hard.

"I can answer that," Jade said. "When we passed through the membrane of the parallel world, he was healed of existing injuries. But when we were ejected back into this reality we were at the mercy of gravity and he hit his head when the cars crashed. And your mom was probably king-hit by the airbag like Callie and I."

Everyone looked at Jade.

"Don't you know anything about quantum physics? It's the healing part that really confuses me," she said. "And don't look at me for answers," she said, looking directly at Callie. "It's your son who can manipulate time and space."

"How did we get here?" Sally asked Daniel, ignoring Jade as if she found her words baffling.

"Right now, your guess is as good as mine," Daniel said, watching Kevin, Tim and Alex walk up the veranda steps to the house. Kevin fished the spare key out of the hanging flowerpot and opened the front door.

"How about we get our things inside? We also need to separate these cars. We can talk about this when our nerves have calmed, and we can rationally analyze the situation." Daniel lifted the cover off the back of the Dodge and started unloading. Shaun stood next to him. "Why don't you go inside with the others and take it easy? Just don't fall asleep for a few hours."

"No, I want to help. My hands don't hurt. I can't believe it. There is a place where everything can be healed. How did it happen?" He raised his eyes up and looked directly into Daniel's. "My dad believed there was such a place. I thought he was just ..." Shaun looked away.

Daniel saw the pain. "I'm not going to lie to you. I don't know, mate. I'm just as confused as you. I thank God we're alive. What was that thing chasing us? I have never seen anything like it in my life."

"It's from hell," Shaun said.

"Well, it has to have come from somewhere, but I'm not sure that hell is the answer. You want to take this?" Daniel handed over the cardboard box of canned and packet foods.

"It is. I was there — when the gates were opened ten years ago in the Middle East."

Daniel stopped and looked at Shaun, not sure what he was talking about. Shaun was struggling to reveal something he had kept hidden for a very long time.

"He took me on a dig. He was an archaeologist, my dad. My mom was dying and he believed he had found a cure. A world where there was no pain and suffering. Immortality. He called it heaven on earth. He blew up ten men along with a young girl, Rachel, to have that artefact. But then he sold it to a prince, or a Russian oil tycoon in Egypt, I'm not sure. I am only starting to recall what happened and piece the memories together. I thought he just wanted the money for medicine." *There were two flights, not one,* he remembered. "My dad argued with the buyer about something. I was drugged most of the time, lying on a red and gold silky daybed, but occasionally I woke to hear my dad yelling, begging them to let him use the artefact, to open the door to a place that would heal his dying wife. My father carried me as they escorted us off the premises, shoving us into a limo and driving us to the airport."

Jade couldn't help her curiosity, but now wished she had gone in with the others. Daniel seemed as if he didn't know what to say to Shaun. She felt he was telling the truth. Maybe some of the story was confused in Shaun's mind because he was young and fragile when something extraordinary happened to him and now he believed all of it to be true memories. She watched Shaun pull out a bulging leather pouch and pour the contents into his hand.

"I think they somehow needed these too."

Jade couldn't see.

"They fell out of Dad's backpack to the Jeep's floor and I took them."

Kookaburras laughed, crows cawed and the smell of cow manure suddenly overwhelmed Jade's senses. Shaun tipped the contents back into the pouch and shoved them deep into his front pocket.

"Be careful you don't lose them. They would be worth a fair bit. You shouldn't carry them around."

"Sure." Shaun took the boxes from Daniel and walked up the porch stairs.

NIGHT WAS FALLING by the time they had dinner, cleaned up and were settled for the evening. In the living room, Shaun was playing a game of jacks with Alex on the rug using the stones from his pocket. He scooped them up off the floor as soon as Daniel walked into the room. "Where's Kevin?"

"He went outside to the hangar to show off the plane to Jade. I think he's got a thing for her. Has he really flown it?"

"Yeah, Callie's dad taught him as soon as he could see out the window. He's a pretty awesome dude. Why don't you guys get along?"

"I don't know." Shaun closed up and walked out of the house.

"Come on, little guy, it's past your bedtime." Alex jumped up into Daniel's arms and hugged him tight.

"I don't want to sleep alone. I'm scared the angry giant is going to pull the roof off the house when I'm sleeping, and stick his hand inside and search through the rooms until he finds me. Shaun said that he would sleep with me and stab its hand if it tried to get me. But he just left, where is he going?"

"He's just gone to get some fresh air. How about I stay with you until he comes back?" Daniel carried Alex to bed. He nudged open the bedroom door with his foot and laid him down on the bed.

"No, not this bed! Shaun said he would sleep in this bed in case it comes through the door and he will attack it so I can run away."

"Okay, buddy," he said, laying Alex on the other single bed. He closed the window and the shutters. Alex was making him aware of his own fears. *I suppose we are all going to be a little jumpy and afraid for a while.* Daniel lay on the bed, sharing the pillow with Alex, and started to tell him a story about the time when Alex had visited his nanna and pop in the school holidays with Callie and Kevin. "Early in the morning, Kevin showed you how to milk the cow. When you were finished, he pulled two straws out of his back pocket and gave you one. Together you sat in the barn on the hay drinking the warm milk." Daniel felt Alex's breathing settle into a peaceful rhythm. The door squeaked open and Shaun popped his head in. Daniel waved for him to come in and turned on the bedside light and whispered, "Are you okay?"

"Yeah, tired. I'm going to hit the pillow," Shaun said.

"I'll come in and check on you both later. Thanks for your help today."

"You don't need to check on me," Shaun said, lying on the bed with his back to Daniel.

"Night." Daniel left the bedside light on and quietly walked out.

AT THE FAR end of the sweeping wooden veranda that stretched around the country home Jade sat in an egg-shaped white cane chair that was hanging from the roof. Jade had her feet tucked up on the seat and she rested her chin on her knees. She studied her toes, thinking of her parents. Her contact lenses were annoying her but she resisted the urge to rub. Kath and Sally had made themselves comfortable sitting on a cane sofa.

"Mobile phones are useless these days," Kath said to Sally. "We can't just stay here, we have to do something."

A warm morning breeze gently lifted Jade's raven hair as she vacated her solitary chair. She went inside and the screen door closed quietly by itself. Jade agreed with Kath, having tried to call her dad six times this morning, without success. She went to the bathroom to dry her eyes and adjust her contact lenses. She thought about Kevin and couldn't help believing that he could help her get back to her dad and find her mom.

It had now been a couple of days since they had arrived and everyone was on edge. Kevin had asked his dad if they could go for a walk up Saddleback Mountain later today, saying it was important, but he didn't know why.

Jade could hear the boys at the back of the house, and Daniel and Callie were in the kitchen cleaning up from breakfast. The house reminded her of her own home, just a lot bigger. She closed the bathroom door. Her eyes were irritated from crying and she fished out her contact lenses. Sitting on the edge of the toilet seat she grabbed her stomach as if in physical pain, then dropped her head forward and cried. Her tears splashed onto the blue and white tiles. Jade hardly moved for ten minutes, letting it all out. She felt her mind becoming distracted, intrigued by the way her tears had landed in between the tiles and falling close enough together to dampen the grout. How random ... but no, it wasn't random, was it? Because her posture and lack of movement created the same pathway for each tear to fall. It gave her some sense of relief to see order amongst the chaos. "S = k log W," she said aloud. "S = k log W."

Bang, bang, bang. "How long are you going to be in there? I've got to do a number two," Alex's muffled voice said.

"Coming out now." She flushed the toilet and washed her face and hands.

"Hurry, I can feel it popping out like a turtle head."

"That's disgusting, Alex." She pulled open the door and held it for him, but he didn't rush in.

"Are you sad?"

"No, just dirt in my eyes."

"That's what Kevin says too."

"I thought you were busting?"

"Is it going to smell? Do I have to hold my breath?"

"Is what going to smell?" Jade said.

"In there," he said, pointing inside the bathroom. "You were in there for such a long time you must have done a number two."

"No, it's not going to smell," she said. A smile crept across her face and she gave him a little push inside the bathroom. Just before the door closed, Alex yelled, "Oh, K's looking for you."

Jade walked down the long hallway towards the back of the house and out to the veranda. It was peaceful and everything looked so ordinary, it was hard to believe the world was falling apart. She had to stop thinking like that; it didn't help anyone. Focus on sifting through the disorder to find order. She leant against the rail and looked out across the fields. The hangar side door boomed as Shaun slammed it behind him.

"And stay away from my brother," Kevin yelled.

Jade watched Shaun turn around and lunge at Kevin and suddenly they were both on the ground wrestling. She jumped over the wooden rail. "Stop it, you two," she said, coming up beside them. Tim came running over and pulled at Kevin. Jade pulled at Shaun's shirt.

"Stop it," she said.

Daniel came up behind her and pulled Jade off Shaun. "What's going on here? All of you over here, park yourselves on the steps."

Kevin dug his elbow into Shaun's ribs as he got up and as he went to the steps Shaun smacked him up the back of the head.

"Enough, you two. Kevin, what's going on? Why don't you two get along?"

"I don't know, Dad."

"Yes, you do, don't give me that."

"Maybe you would like to explain, Shaun?"

"He's a bully," Tim said. "He beats up on anyone who pisses him off and has a fascination for petrol bombs."

"Shut up!" Shaun said, swiping at Tim.

"How do you know this, Tim? Think carefully before you answer. I have only seen Shaun helping out since he has been here with us. He has paid more attention to Alex than you, Kevin. He has just lost his father in a fire and you are accusing him of being a firebug. Did you see him start any fires?"

"Well, no, because —" Tim said.

"So you didn't see him start any. Did he tell you he started any?"

"No, but —"

"But what?"

"I was there."

"You were at the scene of the fire?"

"We were down at the river when we saw Shaun and his entourage leave the area just before it went up," Kevin said. "That's all."

"We need to work together, guys. You both have seen what happens if you give in to urges of violence. Nobody wins, we all lose. For the rest of the day I want you two to work together. Whatever your differences are, or what you think each other has done, you leave behind now and you start to care for one another. I know it sounds gross, but try it. You understand what I'm saying? Kevin — Shaun?"

Jade watched Kevin and Shaun avoid looking at each other until the tension seemed to ease as Kevin relaxed.

"Sure, Dad. I'm sorry, we all deserve a second chance."

"Shaun?"

"Yeah."

"Okay, pack a couple of backpacks and we will take that hike up the mountain."

Jade stood up and Kevin followed with Tim. "Wait up, guys," Daniel said to Kevin and Shaun, still sitting on the veranda steps. "Together. If one of you is in the toilet I want to see the other one standing outside the door waiting. Got the picture?"

Jade found the image funny and quickly turned away. Shaun stood up and fell into step with them.

"Why do you guys dislike each other?" Jade asked.

"It's nothing," Kevin said.

"Nothing!" Tim said.

"He broke my leg, crushed my knee. He is a maniac," Tim burst out.

"I knew I broke it!" Shaun said, as if a puzzle had just been solved. "I heard it crack, but then when I fell off the roof I saw you standing next to me. I couldn't work it out."

"There, he admitted it," Tim said, looking at Jade. "I told you he broke my leg."

"Is that when you went into the parallel world to escape the fire?" Jade asked. "If it is, that explains why you saw him walking around, Shaun. He had been healed. Isn't that amazing? You could create a space for the sick to walk through — like opening and closing a door — as long as they work out why they are sick in the first place, because everything has a cause and effect. Like what's happening around the world. There has to be a root cause somewhere that we can go back to and correct."

Shaun looked at Tim's leg again and back at Jade and she thought he was going to cry.

Instead, he said, "Well don't give me reason to do it again," and walked off. Kevin followed him and Tim stayed with Jade.

11

SEEDS OF EXISTENCE: CASEY. ENGLAND

Casey waited, sitting at the bottom of the stairs, for one of them to wake up. It was after three in the afternoon and they had been sleeping all day.

He wanted to burst into Sophia's room and check she was still there. Twice Amy caught him trying to quietly open the door to take a peek, and twice she scolded him with just a look, ushering him downstairs to this very spot an hour ago.

"You're going to have to come up with a name for that dog," Amy said. "Come on, let's go for a walk."

"Where to? It's not safe," Casey said.

She held out her hand to him. "Come on." Casey took it and allowed her to lead him through the living room into the kitchen and out the back door. The dog came running out of the woods, glad to see them. The wind had a sharp chill, their breath was frosty. Winter had crept up on the calendar. They approached the edge of the woods and waited for the dog to catch up.

"I was thinking of calling her Lucy," Casey said, dropping to his knees. The dog licked his face and Casey wrapped his right arm around its neck, giving it a rough pat and a scratch along its back.

"After your mom. That would be perfect."

"Why?" Casey asked.

"Because ever since this dog showed up it has done what it could to protect you, just as your mom would."

"I haven't decided yet." Casey looked down at his boots as they walked.

"I'm sorry about the other day," Amy said. "I am so sorry. I don't know what came over me. At first I thought I had the virus and that frightened me so much. I was worrying about you and Terry and the baby."

"Babies! And it's okay, I get it," he said. "I know you're sorry. The twins will make you smile."

She bit her bottom lip, hesitated and in a soft voice she asked, "What do you see?"

"One image, just one image, of you wearing a white summer dress, sitting on your knees on a picnic blanket on green grass trying to control two babies determined to crawl all over you. You are laughing. They are giggling and climbing over you and you nearly lose your balance and have to throw your hands behind you for support, while they continue to keep climbing. One is trying to suck your chin. I can't quite tell if it is two boys, or a boy and a girl. One is definitely a boy. You are very happy."

"What about you and Terry, and everyone else?"

"I don't know, that's all I see," Casey said.

She put her arm around him and gave him a squeeze and kissed his head. "You still need that haircut." He put his arm around her and together they walked to the front of the house.

They came across Father McDonald on his knees on the ground, praying, his eyes closed. *When did he wake up?* Casey approached Father McDonald and knelt beside him. Amy did the same so that they were all side by side. Casey closed his eyes and imagined an angel hovering above, ready to take their prayers up to God.

"May your light shine upon us Lord, and enter our hearts so we may be filled with your mercy and strength. I pray ..."

Casey listened to Father McDonald pray and his body filled with effervescent light. He was unaware the prayer had finished. He was still on his knees, but felt the movement of sand under his feet and between his toes. His mother was walking next to him, pointing to the eastern star in the sky. It was dawn and it was the only star, the sun not quite woken from its slumber. He thought he caught a glimpse of a man wearing robes and a funny nightcap, with a ginger beard. He vanished as soon as Casey tried to focus on him. His mom told him of things to come, and that people needed to dare to dream. She talked of him growing up into a man and how he was to teach the others when he was of age. But not once did he see her lips move or hear her voice. They walked in silence and after watching the gentle rhythm of the whitecaps she was gone, the feeling of the sand was gone, the ocean and the morning star, all gone. His knees started to feel the ground beneath him, his ears heard the sound of Amy's voice. He took in a deep breath and opened his eyes. His face was wet with tears, but he didn't recall crying or why. The images faded as a dream fades, their meaning passing, like the sweet fragrance of flowers in a garden. He looked up to see Father McDonald and Amy talking, waiting patiently for him to come around.

"Sophia is often doing this," Father McDonald said. "You just have to be patient and wait for them to return."

"Return from where?" Amy asked.

Casey cleared his throat and said, "I'm right here, I haven't gone anywhere. I may have dozed off but I can still hear you." He got to his feet. "Why were you out here praying? Couldn't you have done it just as well inside?"

"Casey don't be rude, he can pray wherever he likes."

"No, I didn't mean anything by it."

"It's actually a good question. I was outside for a reason. I was reading paragraphs for protection. We are all in great danger of losing our souls. Our bodies are always destined to return to the earth, but our soul is for eternity. If we lose that we will be outside the gates of heaven forever."

"Great, just when I was starting to feel a little better," Joe said from behind.

Casey spun around and there she was standing next to Joe wearing Amy's jeans and sweater. Her hair was in a plait that draped over her shoulder.

"You remind me of someone," Amy said to Sophia.

Sophia smiled at Amy as she walked closer to Casey. They fell into step and walked away from the adults.

"Where are you two off to, hen?" Joe asked.

Casey had to wait for his brain to interpret the accent. But before he could reply, Amy said, "Don't go into the woods or past the garage, and don't let the dog out of your sight."

"Lucy, here, girl," Sophia called to the dog and it ran up to her and sat down in front of her. Its tail dusted the ground waiting for praise. Amy and Casey held each other's gaze. Casey pulled away first.

"Why did you call the dog Lucy, Sophia?" Amy asked.

"Isn't that its name?"

Amy looked at Casey, Sophia looked at Casey, they both waited for an answer.

"Yeah, her name is Lucy."

"Okay, then that's settled. Lucy it is," Amy said. "Dinner will be ready in an hour," she said, reaching to touch Joe's shoulder. "Come on, I bet you're famished," she said.

Casey felt a sense of gratitude towards Amy. Father McDonald, Amy and Joe wandered inside the house and the smells of Terry's stew came drifting out as they opened and closed the back door.

"Hmm, that man can cook," was the last thing Casey heard. He was alone with Sophia for the first time since she had arrived. Now that they were together and alone he didn't know what to say or do. He could feel she was feeling a little strange too. He felt her hand brush his and he gently took it.

PIGEONS COOED in the loft and light streamed through the rafters. Sophia passed an eye over the items in the barn and sat on the motorcycle. She leant forward, holding onto the handlebars and said, "We have to meet up with the others, although I can't see how it's going to happen."

"We can chill and wait a day or two and see what happens," Casey said. "I keep coming back to this one thought: we are all that is, all that was, and ever will be. We carry all the seeds of all existence. From the stars in the sky to the table in the kitchen to the pain in our hearts, we are the light and the darkness."

"You're right. Can you see how we meet the others? I think we will come together when we least expect it, but sometimes I just want to know. It can be so annoying at times not knowing, but sort of knowing, if you get what I mean. Can you start this motorcycle?"

"I get it." He didn't need to be asked twice. He directed

his energy smoothly over to the motorcycle and it roared into life.

Sophia's body tensed. She smiled in joy and trepidation. "That's so awesome," she said. "I have never been able to do anything like that. I can feel its power. It would be marvelous to go for a ride." He watched as her energy expanded with joy and excitement.

"Can we take it for a ride?"

"I ... I don't think so."

"Oh, come on. Just out the front and back," Sophia said.

"Okay, why not? We're probably going to die anyway, might as well have fun."

She climbed off the bike and pushed him. "Don't say that. Take it back, right now! We're not going to die Casey." She gently put her hand on the side of his head. "It's all in here, remember. If you think you will be defeated, then that's what you will be — defeated. If you think you will be successful, then you will be successful. Put out negative thoughts, you get negative results. Put out positive thoughts and you get positive results. Simple. If you don't believe me, try it."

"Sorry, I didn't mean it the way it sounded," Casey said, defending himself.

"Nobody does. I know. You have to put consciousness into each thought, otherwise you become a drifter and then you are open to all sorts. That's better, your aura just changed. Now I can see flashes of emerald-green, peachy-orange and violet. You balanced yourself, excellent. Let's go for that ride."

"Do you always see auras? I don't."

"No, not always, and I have worked hard not to see. It's paying off."

"You will have to get off while I push it out."

He wheeled the Bonneville backwards out of the garage and climbed on. He held it steady while Sophia threw her leg over the back. She held onto the passenger side-bars. Casey wished she would hold onto him. He slowly let out the clutch. It revved out in first gear, but it didn't matter. Casey worked out the clutch and how to shift into second. The bike jerked and accelerated a little faster down to the gate. They skidded slightly at the fence. Slowly, Casey maneuvered the motorbike and did a wide U-turn. He saw Terry on the back steps with his hands on his hips. Casey rode slowly up to him.

"My turn!" Terry said.

Casey had been sure Terry was going to be cross. "No worries, she's all yours," he said, putting the motorcycle in neutral.

Terry held the bike still while Casey and Sophia dismounted. Terry popped the stand down with his foot. Climbed on and flicked it back up. He gave the Bonneville a couple of revs and took off. It wasn't long before Joe came out and wanted a turn. Amy sat on the step with Father McDonald and watched. It was Casey's turn again and this time he went solo and felt the freedom, the wind in his hair. He felt alive. Casey settled into the seat and the joy and freedom of riding. He could have headed out the drive and down the road and just kept going.

"You know you have to wear protective gear next time!" Amy yelled.

"What about me?" Sophia called.

Casey circled back. Sophia was grinning with excitement and hopped on as soon as he pulled up. This time she put her arms around his waist. Butterflies danced in his stomach, his face felt like he had stepped into a sauna. Anxious to have the wind cool his face he put the bike into first and turned to ride back to the front gate. *Another great feeling; being on a motorcycle,* he thought. *It couldn't get better than this.*

Having fun was energizing. After the adults finished playing with the bike Casey and Sophia had one more turn, then parked it in the garage. Casey kicked an old coaster under the stand after he positioned the bike just right.

Sophia waited and fiddled with the odds and ends in the barn. "While I was on the back of the motorcycle," she said, "I saw us riding again. We weren't alone, and I don't mean Joe and Terry. Those from the other side of the world are going to have a turn on your Bonneville. They are coming to us."

IT HAD BEEN A LONG DAY. After spending last night in the basement, Casey was extremely tired. He didn't want to sleep, though, and he was worried that when he woke, Sophia would be gone and it had just been a dream. But his eyes were not going to stay open unless he pinned them to his eyebrows. They were all sitting in the lounge room and he had his legs flung over the arm of the chair next to the bookshelves. Amy and Terry had their legs curled up on the sofa. Father McDonald and Joe sat in the armchairs facing them. Sophia was only an arm's length away, the coffee table with the lamp on it between them; it was the only thing separating the pair. He tried to focus on the conversations. He grew more and more tired. The lights started to flicker, he floated into a restless sleep, and was unaware Amy and Terry were now standing by his side.

ACKNOWLEDGMENT

I would like to thank my high school English teacher and my supportive family and friends for their encouragements. Thank you, to the invaluable editors, Linda Funnell and Stephanie Smith who have been a tremendous support. No book is complete without the vital service of editors, proof-readers and great book cover designers. Finally, I would like to acknowledge the professional project management services of Joel Naoum from Critical Mass, who made it possible to share my story with you.

ABOUT JM HART

Now semi-retired, JM moved to a peaceful county town south of Sydney, to focus on her grandchildren and writing.

JM Hart is the author of The Emerald Tablet Series, and The Chronicles of the Supernatural. She makes her online home at http://jmhartwriter.com

You can also connect with JM Hart (Jeanette) on:

Facebook, Instagram, Pinterest and Twitter.

And you should send her an email at author@jmhartwriter.com if the mood strikes you.

GLOSSARY

Al-mawet – Mawet means death, al-mawet is no death. The spelling varies within different religious text, but they all have the same meaning.

Arrow of time – the direction of events; movement in time is generally forward.

Athanasia – means timelessness, everlasting life. Athanasia is referred to as the parallel world/dimension.

Dark matter – a negative energy force. In this story the dark matter also contains micro shapeshifting demons.

Dovesti zhenshchinu – pronunciation for Russian довести женщину. English translation: bring the woman.

Dunny – toilet.

Fair dinkum – an expression in Australian slang proclaiming a truth about a statement.

Intel – slang for intelligent person. As in geek. (Created by the author)

Merkaba – two tetrahedrons combined. Mystically it is a channel for the descending energy of the universe and the ascending energy of Earth. Spiritual tool of transformation.

Metatron's Cube – a geometric shape/solid. It has thirteen equal circles. Lines from the center of each circle extend out to the centers of the other 12 circles.

Outback – A remote area of the country.

Platonic Solids – shapes with equal sides. The five platonic solids are; tetrahedron hexahedron, octahedron, dodecahedron and icosahedron.

S=k log W – the second law of thermodynamics. Entropy – a mathematical formula that represents the lack of order or predictability. A slow decline into disorder or randomness. (Our characters want to reverse this state of being or create a new one from the disorder the negative thoughts of man and the micro beasts have created.)

Sphere – a round solid with equal distance from its center.

Stickybeak – an overly inquisitive person.

Talking stick – a ceremonial stick that is passed around a group of people giving the holder the right to speak.

The devil's puppets – the people controlled by the micro demons. Those infected by the virus which is the dark matter.

The Tree of Life – a spiritual concept that has been used and referred to throughout the centuries in mythology, religion and philosophy to name but a few. It refers to the interconnection of life and its evolution.

Vremaya dlya distsipliny – Russian pronunciation for Время для дисциплины. English translation: time for discipline (a good whipping in this story).

If you enjoyed the first book in the Emerald Tablet Series, please go to www.jmhartwriter.com for the next book.

Enjoy this book? You can make a big difference

Reviews are the most powerful tools in my arsenal when it comes getting attention for my books. Much as I'd like to, I don't have the financial muscle of a New York publisher. I can't take out full page ads in the newspaper or put posters on the subway.

(Not yet, anyway).

But I do have something much more powerful and effective than that, and it's something that those publishers would kill to get their hands on.

A committed and loyal bunch of readers.

Honest reviews of my books help bring them to the attention of other readers.

If you've enjoyed this book I would be very grateful if you could spend just five minutes leaving a review (it can be as short as you like) on the your favorite online bookstore, which you can access through my website as well as BOOK THREE, THE FINAL BOOK in the serial. https://jmhartwriter.com/buy-now/

Thank you very much.